John Dougherty

Bansi O'Hara and the Bloodline Prophecy

Illustrated by James de la Rue

CORGI YEARL

BANSI O'HARA AND THE BLOODLINE PROPHECY
A CORGI YEARLING BOOK 978 0 440 86787 6

Published in Great Britain by Corgi Yearling,
an imprint of Random House Children's Books
A Random House Group Company

This edition published 2008

1 3 5 7 9 10 8 6 4 2

The Random House Group Limited makes every effort to ensure that the papers used in its books are made from trees that have been legally sourced from well-managed and credibly certified forests. Our paper procurement policy can be found at: www.randomhouse.co.uk/paper.htm

Corgi Yearling Books are published by Random House Children's Books,
61–63 Uxbridge Road, London W5 5SA

www.**kidsatrandomhouse**.co.uk
www.rbooks.co.uk

Addresses for companies within The Random House Group Limited can be found at: www.randomhouse.co.uk/offices.htm

THE RANDOM HOUSE GROUP Limited Reg. No. 954009

A CIP catalogue record for this book is available from the British Library.

Printed and bound in Great Britain by CPI Bookmarque,
Croydon, CR0 4TD

To Noah & Cara, with all my love.
And to Ravi & Niamh, who first inspired
the idea that became Bansi,
with much love from your uncle John.

Acknowledgements

Thanks go first and foremost to my beautiful Kate, for supporting and encouraging me in my writing even when the dishes are piling up in the sink waiting for me to wash them; and to my fantastic children, Noah and Cara, for lending Daddy to the computer keyboard long enough for me to get this finished, for the interest you take in my work, and for just being you. I love you.

Thanks to my wonderful agent, Sarah Molloy at A.M. Heath & Co, for all the support, advice, guidance and encouragement.

And, of course, thanks to everyone at Random House Children's Books, especially: to Annie Eaton for her calmness in the face of an author's self-induced crisis and for not holding it against me(!); to Lucy Walker for her assiduous and at times challenging attention to detail (publishing's loss is very much the law's gain; I shall miss working with you); Laura Harris (in advance) for all the hard work that, as I write, is yet to come; and above all to Sue Cook, who first spotted the potential in both Bansi and in me, and without whom neither of us might ever have made it into print.

Thank you all!

Bansi O'Hara
and the
Bloodline Prophecy

Chapter One

High on a hillside, in the grey half-darkness that comes before dawn, a raven was listening.

It was listening to the sound of the wind stirring the branches of the ancient tree in which it sat; for the wind, as it sighed and breathed and sorrowed through the boughs, was singing.

The raven was a very old bird, and it recognized the song, having heard it many times across the centuries. It cawed harshly and shook its black-feathered wings, making itself a ragged silhouette against the cold, eerie gloom. Then it folded itself small, as if hiding from something that was to come.

If you had been there that morning, as on the far side of the hill the first light of Midsummer's Eve began its slow creeping march over the distant horizon, you would have felt a magical stillness settle all around. The whispering song of the wind became a murmuring, then a humming which would have filled your head as if it came from inside you. The ancient standing stones that encircled the tree took on a strange glow, one which could not entirely be explained by the coming sunrise; the grass between them seemed suddenly to grow a little, becoming greener and brighter even in the half-light of dawn.

And a shape – which you would have sworn hadn't been there a moment before – unfolded, like a flower opening up, into the form of a young boy dressed in clothes the colours of shimmering flame. A small, dark, almost human figure, difficult to make out clearly in the dim half-light, perched on his shoulder.

The boy stepped out of the stone circle. He looked down at the awakening village in the valley, and a broad grin split his handsome face. With a sudden whoop of joy he leaped up high, higher than you have ever seen anyone leap, twisting and turning and tumbling like an acrobat in the air.

The boy's small companion cursed angrily. He clung desperately with his long wiry fingers, his legs flailing and scrabbling in vain for a foothold. Then, with a yell, he fell off.

'Urggh!' he spluttered, picking himself up and spitting out a mouthful of dry earth. 'I suppose you think that was funny!'

The boy, alighting, squatted down and looked into the little brown man's eyes. 'Let me think, now,' he said, his own eyes glinting roguishly. 'Hmmm . . . yep, I'd say that was definitely funny. All the elements of a good gag. It's well you have me here to keep you right about these things, Pogo.'

Pogo scowled angrily. Wrinkle upon wrinkle creased and crammed into the thousands already covering his small, leathery face.

'This is no time for games and foolishness, Tam!' he growled. 'We're not the only ones after the Blood of the Morning Stars! You can bet your life there'll be someone following us any moment – and it's not just your own life you'll be betting, either,' he added, his face almost disappearing into the wrinkles as his frown grew deeper. 'It's all our lives you're wagering with your foolery. Yours, mine, Caithne's – the lives of everyone who's risked the anger of the Dark Lord. And worse still – the life we're here to protect.'

Tam laughed softly. 'Listen to yourself, Pogo,' he teased. 'It's all worry and the end of the world with you, isn't it? We'll be fine!'

'Do you not realize how important this is?' the little man hissed furiously. 'How many lives depend upon it? How the whole future of—'

'Ah, come on, Pogo,' Tam grinned. 'It's me who's done all the work so far. I got us here safely, and ahead of anyone else, didn't I? It's up to you for the next bit. You're the expert on mortals and their ways, after all.'

Pogo glared at him. 'Hold your whisht, then!' he snapped. 'And hold still!' With one wiry hand, he laid hold of Tam's hair and, with no attempt at all to be gentle, climbed up on the boy's shoulders. 'Now,' he continued, 'get to the high ground!'

The rise of the hillside almost levelled out under the stone circle, but above it the ground rose sharply and quickly to the top. Tam, his good humour undented by Pogo's temper, leaped to his feet and sprinted swiftly up the steep grassy slope with no more effort than if he were running downhill. Nearing the summit, he sprang into the air. Pogo gripped tightly, but this time there were no acrobatics. The leap brought them down perfectly on the hilltop.

'Hey!' Tam exclaimed in surprise, staring at his feet. 'What's this?'

Pogo looked down at the hard, coarse black surface and then at the wooden railings that almost surrounded them. 'It's called a . . . car park,' he said, concentrating. 'The mortals come up here in their cars to admire the view.'

'What's a car then?' Tam asked.

Pogo ignored him. 'Quiet!' He stood, scanning the horizon all around – to the west, and the retreating shadows of night; to the north, towards the distant mountains that blocked the sea from view; to the east, and the warm glow of the rising sun; to the south . . . and then back to the south-east, where far in the distance something was moving.

'There!' He pointed with a twig-like finger towards the long road into the valley.

Tam's sharp eyes made out a pair of red tail-lights, miles off and moving rapidly further away.

'That, Tam, is a car.' Pogo paused, as if listening. '*The* car. The one that will fetch the mortal child who has the Blood of the Morning Stars, both streams reunited at last, flowing through her veins. By night-fall, she'll be within reach of the gate. And it's up to us to make sure nothing from beyond the gate reaches out and takes her,' he added darkly. 'If we're up to the task.'

Tam clearly shared none of his small companion's forebodings. Letting out a triumphant yell, he bent his knees and hurled himself at the sky. High into the air he leaped, and this time he did not come down.

His arms stretched out wide as he rose, broadening and feathering. His neck elongated; a soft whiteness bloomed and blossomed over his head and body until – without it being possible to tell exactly how – he was no longer a wild and handsome boy, but a magnificent swan. Pogo, legs and arms wrapped tightly round the swan's neck, crouched low between its wings as they took to the skies. They wheeled, sweeping in a wide arc over the hillside, and followed the distant tail-lights.

If you had been there, watching on the hill as the swan-that-was-not-a-swan passed high over the stone circle, you would have seen another shape unfold in the fading shadows under the tree – a second boy, older and crueller in appearance than Tam and dressed in dark clothes made of animal-skin. Over his shoulders was draped a rough, hairy cloak made of a single untrimmed pelt. Its macabre hood was an empty scalp, with pricked ears and canine muzzle, which hung gruesomely upside-down behind him and stared sightlessly at an inverted sky.

Unseen, the newcomer raised his eyes and hungrily observed the departing swan. Reaching behind him, he grasped his hood and pulled it sharply over his head, entirely covering his face. With one flowing movement he drew the cloak firmly around him; it clung and enveloped him, changing and moulding and stretching, its dangling legs tightly wrapping around his limbs. The grisly hood hardened as if within it a skull was somehow forming, ossifying over the boy's own face; its dead, glassy eyes suddenly gleamed with life and swivelled chillingly as if in search of something.

A moment later you would have seen no boy at all, but a great grey wolf which raised its huge head menacingly. For a moment longer it gazed after the swan, and then bounded from the circle in faster pursuit than you would have thought possible.

The raven ruffled its feathers and tipped its head to one side as it watched them go.

'Bloomin' 'eck,' it muttered to itself. 'Here we go again!'

Chapter Two

It was a beautiful morning. The sun shone with a gentle promise of warmth, drawing out the strong colours of the Irish summer.

Anyone walking along the narrow country road towards the sleepy village of Ballyfey that morning could, if they were sharp-eyed and quiet, have caught a glimpse of a solitary badger returning late to its sett. They might, had the mood taken them, have lingered to watch the glossy chestnut mare cantering across her wide green field, or to listen to the lone thrush singing in the sycamore tree. They would probably, if they were in no hurry, have stopped to gaze up in awe and wonder at the sight of a majestic white swan beating its solitary way across the sky.

They would definitely, if they valued their lives, have leaped headlong into the prickly hawthorn hedge as the dark green Morris Minor Traveller roared round the bend on the wrong side of the narrow road at a speed something in excess of eighty miles per hour.

And as they emerged again, scratched and bleeding, they might have heard the sound of two elderly ladies screaming their heads off at each other, before the car carried them out of earshot.

'Nora Maura Margaret Mullarkey, will you *slow down*?'

'Ah, be quiet, you silly old trout!'

'Be quiet yourself, you lunatic, and slow down before you kill us both!'

'Don't be daft, Eileen. Kill us? Sure, we're as safe as houses with me at the wheel, and you know it.'

'Safe as houses, is it? What houses are there that're safe with *you* driving around? You nearly knocked the front room out of Michael Brennan's in the last village!'

'Well, it shouldn't have been there! What kind of a silly place is that to build a house, I ask you!'

'Nora, it's been there for over *four hundred years*! You can't just decide it's in the wrong place because you want to drive on the footpath all of a sudden!'

'Weren't you the one who wanted us to get there in good time?'

'I'd rather get there alive, if it's all the same to—*LOOK OUT!!!*'

The car screeched to a halt, its bumper inches from the side of a large black-and-white cow.

The cow turned slowly to look at them, rather like a teacher who has just caught you running in the corridors for the five hundredth time this year and really doesn't know if he can be bothered to tell you off *again*.

'Moooo,' it observed.

It stood idly in the middle of the road, surrounded on its other three sides by what looked like all its friends and extended family plus a good-sized helping of distant relatives.

'Mmmoooo,' agreed a few of the others, staring at the car for a moment and then shaking their heads sorrowfully.

The car window squeaked with disgust as Nora Mullarkey wound it down and stuck her head out.

'Sean! Sean McKnight! Where are you, you daft great lump?' she yelled.

There was a wriggling movement from somewhere in the hedge and a thin, pale young man emerged, pulling thorns from his skin and examining the fresh tears in his clothing.

'Sean!' Mrs Mullarkey snapped. 'What do you think you're doing, messing about in that hedge when you should be getting these cows off the road? Come on, now!'

Sean blinked, brushed a few leaves and an abandoned bird's nest from his head, and ambled over to the car.

'Morning,' he said.

'Don't you "morning" *me*, you young hooligan. Leaving these cows all over the road where anyone could run into them while you go off fooling around in hedges!'

Sean grinned ruefully at Mrs Mullarkey's passenger. 'Morning, Mrs O'Hara! Where might you be off to? Anywhere nice?'

'We're just off to collect my son, Fintan, and his family from the boat. If Nora's driving doesn't kill us all first, of course.' Mrs O'Hara cast a look at her friend. 'A fine thing that would be, bringing them over here from London for all our funerals!'

Mrs Mullarkey bristled. 'Funerals, is it, Mrs High-and-Mighty O'Hara?'

'High-and-Mighty? What do you mean by that, Nora Mullarkey?'

'What, are you going to tell me now that your family *isn't* descended from the High Kings of Donegal like you're always crowing about, then?'

'Well, and so what if we are? Can I help it if my family has an illustrious heritage? And one that I don't want to see ending in little pieces all over the road in the middle of a herd of cows!'

'I stopped, didn't I? Which is more than I can say for you, going on about your blessed High Kings of Donegal all the time . . .'

Sean sighed, shook his head and turned back to the cows. 'Ho, there! Come on, now!' he called, and the cattle slowly began to lumber off through the gate into the field. Behind him, over the sound of the continuing argument, came the grind and crunch of Mrs Mullarkey finding first gear. He looked round to see the car leap wildly forward, roaring like some fearsome beast, and disappear from view.

Bansi O'Hara could hardly contain her excitement. Granny O'Hara had visited her and her parents in London quite often – and sometimes even came to look after Bansi when her parents' work took them away from home during term-time – but at ten years old this was her first trip to Granny's house in Ballyfey, the house her father had grown up in. She stood at the front of the ship, feeling the cold salt sea spray her face, and strained her eyes to catch her first glimpse of Ireland.

Her father, a tall, curly-haired man with rugged Irish good looks and a permanent twinkle in his eye, leaned on the railing next to her. 'Are we nearly there yet?' he asked teasingly.

Bansi tipped her head accusingly. 'Dad! Be fair! When was the last time I ever said that?'

'Oh . . . about five minutes ago!'

'I did not!' Bansi retorted, scandalized. 'I said no such thing!'

'Ah . . . no, you're right, that was me that time, too, wasn't it?'

'Yes,' said Bansi. 'And the time before that, and the time before *that* as well!'

'No, be fair yourself, the time before that was your mother . . . talking of whom, where's she gone?'

'Right here!' Bansi's mum came up behind them, blinking as the sea-breeze whipped black trails of hair across her pretty round face. Even windswept, and even in her faded denims, she somehow managed to look – as Bansi thought of it – mischievously elegant, as if her beauty refused to take itself seriously. In each slender hand she carried a polystyrene cup of tea. 'I got this for you,' she said, offering one to her husband.

'Asha, my love, you're an angel.' Bansi's dad took the cup and warmed his hands on it, the lines round his eyes creasing in a smile that made him look wise as well as kindly. He glanced up as something in the sky caught his attention. 'Now would you look at that!'

A beautiful white swan was winging its way towards the ferry. The passengers on the deck looked up, shielding their eyes against the day's brightness. Bansi felt her heart leap as she gazed at the creature;

the daylight danced in dazzling reflection across the water, a path to lead the swan straight to the ship – and to her. For a moment she had the feeling of a connection, a line as intangible and yet as real as the sunlight shining on the sea, stretching between herself and the great bird.

'That's something you don't see every day,' Bansi's mum remarked. 'Isn't it lovely?' She smiled down at her daughter; and Bansi smiled back.

The swan turned and kept pace with the ship, just low enough for the little brown man-goblin on its back to get a good view of the passengers without being spotted.

'That's her, Tam!' he said. 'The Child of the Blood of the Morning Stars!'

'Which one?' the swan asked.

Pogo rolled his eyes. 'Don't you know anything about mortals?'

The swan shrugged, and Pogo was thrown suddenly forwards. He cursed, flinging his arms round his companion's neck.

'Watch out!' he snarled. 'Right; now look and listen, so you'll know who it is we're here to protect. Do you see the couple right at the bow end of the deck, looking straight at us – she, brown of skin with black hair that falls around her shoulders; he, light, with sandy curls?'

The swan nodded, and again Pogo was jerked forward. As he clutched at its neck, he was sure he heard it snigger.

'You do that again and I'll boot your next egg back where it came from,' Pogo growled. 'Now: those two are the parents, each descended from one of the two Morning Stars – he from Caer and she from Avalloc. Look at the child beside them: the slender wee girl with golden-brown skin, fairer than her mother's but darker than her father's. Do you see who I mean? She has her mother's black hair, and a face that's strong like her da's but much more elfin. Can't tell from up here which side she gets her eyes from, mind . . .'

'Both,' Tam said immediately. 'They're even larger than the mother's, but the same sort of round almond shape. The grey-green colour's from the da, but they're brighter than his, with a dark rim to the iris. Very striking.'

Pogo started. 'You never saw that from up here?'

'I did. I'm a púca, don't forget. So you reckon that's her? She's very slight, isn't she? I wouldn't give her much odds in a fight. How can you be sure she's the one?'

'I may not have any of what *you'd* call magic,' the little man retorted coldly, 'nor eyesight as sharp as yours either; but I have the instincts of my people. And I know the story of the Morning Stars, too, which is more than it seems you do. Do you not know the story of how Avalloc fled to the ancient forests of India, and Caer to the hills of Donegal? I'm sure, all right. She's the one. I wish I could be half so certain *he* won't get to her before we do.'

Swans can't smile at all, let alone grin broadly, but Tam made the best effort he could. 'How is *that* ever going to happen? Have a bit of sense, Pogo! Come on, admit it – we're way ahead of him.'

Pogo snorted. 'Way ahead of him, indeed,' he muttered. 'Have you forgotten, Tam? It was the Dark Lord's magic that discovered the child was coming within reach of the gate on Midsummer's Eve, not Caithne's. It's only by sheer luck she found out about it at all. If you ask me, we've been trying to catch up with him and his forces all the way.'

Tam chuckled softly. 'Well, we've not only caught them up, we've overtaken them. So stop worrying.'

Beneath the surface of the water, a shape tracked the ship. Fluidly, relentlessly, it moved through the water like some aquatic predator, its focus entirely on the hull that cut through the sea above it.

Had you been there to see it, you might not have recognized it at first, so easily did it move, so naturally did it seem to belong in the undersea environment. You might well have taken it for some strange marine creature. Only as you drew close would you have realized that it was a boy – a dark-haired boy with a cruel, cunning face and no apparent need to breathe. His wolfskin cloak flowed around him like the sea itself, as he cut through the water more swiftly and steadily than a hunting shark.

Chapter Three

Bansi and her parents leaned over the railing, watching the swan. Ahead of them the harbour was now in clear sight, and beyond it Bansi could see hills in the distance, looking somehow wilder and greener than the ones at home. She felt a sudden surge of excitement, so much so that she could hardly keep still, and for want of any other release she hugged her mother tight, making her laugh.

'Tell you what, we're a wee bit ahead,' her dad remarked, glancing at his watch. 'With any luck we might catch the earlier train and be with your granny before tea.'

Bansi's mum put her hand to her mouth. 'Oops!' she said. 'I forgot to tell you! Your mother phoned last night while you were in the shower, to say we needn't take the train. Her friend's bringing her to pick us up . . . What's wrong, love?'

Bansi's dad had gone pale. 'Which friend?'

'Mrs . . . Mullarkey, I think she said. Could that be right?'

Bansi's dad sank his head into his hands and groaned.

'What is it, Dad?' Bansi asked, grinning. Her dad's overacting always amused her. 'She can't be that bad!'

'Ach, no, it's not that, sweetheart. She's very nice, Mrs Mullarkey, in her own way. It's just . . . well, she drives like a maniac. Put her behind the wheel of a car and she goes completely barmy. They've had to armour-plate all the hedgehogs in the county because of her. And the other thing is – well, your granny and Mrs Mullarkey have been friends since they were little girls, and they've somehow never lost that competitive streak that some children have with one another . . .'

The green Morris Minor Traveller screeched into the ferry terminal car park and – its driver utterly ignoring her passenger's frenzied shrieking of, 'Nora, you're going too fast you're going to hit those people WATCH OUT!!!' – came to a surprisingly sudden halt in one and a half parking spaces. After a moment, a couple of nervous-looking pedestrians climbed back down from the roof of the car next to it and hurried away.

'There, now! Didn't I tell you?' Mrs Mullarkey beamed at the world in general. 'Nothing to worry about, and we're here in plenty of time for a cup of tea, too.' She reached into the back of the car for her walking stick and made a great show of leaning on it to help herself out. Not to be outdone, Mrs O'Hara did the same, grasping the top of her stick with both hands. She paused as she stood up, as if in pain but not wanting to complain.

Mrs Mullarkey glared at her for a moment. Then she bent over ever so slightly, as though giving in just a little to a backache she had been heroically struggling against. Mrs O'Hara glared back, winced, bent over just a little more than that and began to limp off towards the terminal.

Mrs Mullarkey groaned, crooked her back a little more and hobbled after her friend, just fast enough to overtake her.

Less than half a minute later, the doors to the ferry terminal burst open. Two little old ladies dashed in, hobbling rather more quickly than the average person is capable of sprinting and both groaning like a pig with an elephant on its head. Their chins practically touching their knees, they bowled over the terminal manager and an entire troop of scouts before screeching to a halt in a dead heat at the tea-shop counter.

Stiffly and with great ceremony, the two women gradually stood upright, pressing down on the tops of their walking sticks. The man behind the counter slowly raised himself from the floor, where he had thrown himself in panic.

'Can I get you anything, ladies?' he asked hesitantly.

Mrs O'Hara turned to her friend. 'You first, Nora,' she said.

'Oh, no, Eileen,' Mrs Mullarkey replied. 'After you, I'm sure.'

Half an hour later, just as the ferry was docking, a soft ripple spread across the water in a secluded bay not far from the harbour. A gull resting on the surface took off in a sudden flurry of panicking wings. Water cascading from his form, the boy with the cruel face emerged from the shallows, inhaling deeply and hungrily but without desperation. Quickly, he drew the hood of the wolfskin over his head and gathered the folds of his cloak around him.

Moments later, the grey wolf turned and sniffed the air.

* * *

'Granny!' shouted Bansi, throwing herself into her grandmother's embrace. 'Granny!'

'Careful, Bansi!' laughed her mother, just as Mrs Mullarkey was saying, 'Now, Eileen, you want to go easy, there. What about your lumbago?'

Bansi's grandmother glared at her friend. 'Lumbago, Nora? Whatever gave you that idea?' She stood up, holding Bansi close to her. 'I've never had trouble with lumbago. It's your own lumbago you need to be careful of.'

Mrs Mullarkey straightened up visibly, to such an extent that behind her the terminal building appeared to be leaning over slightly. 'What *do* you mean, Eileen? Have you forgotten the state you were in when we got here after that long drive? I thought you were never going to stand upright again, your back was giving you such trouble.'

Granny O'Hara bristled. 'What *I* remember, Nora Maura Margaret Mullarkey, is wondering how you could see where you were going, you were so bent over. I felt quite sorry for you, so I did . . .'

'*Sorry?*' repeated Mrs Mullarkey, outraged. '*You* feeling sorry for *me*? Oh, that'll be the day, Eileen, that certainly will . . .'

Bansi looked at her father. 'Told you,' he mouthed.

A few minutes later, a party consisting of a ten-year-old girl, her parents, and the two most vertical elderly ladies ever seen in those parts, made their way across the car park to where Mrs Mullarkey's old green Morris Minor Traveller was waiting for them.

'My goodness, look!' Granny O'Hara suddenly exclaimed as a magnificent white swan flew directly overhead.

'It's following you about, Bansi!' Asha O'Hara teased her daughter. Mrs Mullarkey cast a sharp, enquiring look at them both – but especially at her friend's granddaughter.

Bansi was staring after the bird, dazed by the sudden resurgent feeling of connection that washed over her like a wave. For a moment she felt submerged in a dream, as if the world around her was only half-real, and there was something else beyond it that she could have reached out and touched had she only known how.

'Wakey, wakey, dreamer,' her dad teased, nudging her out of the way as he loaded the luggage into the back of the car. 'We've got a long old trek ahead of us.'

Eileen O'Hara nodded. 'We have that, Fintan.

We'll do a bit of sightseeing on the way, just to break the journey up a bit. Make a day of it. Provided that Nora doesn't break all of us up on the road first with her driving, that is,' she added with a withering look at her friend.

A minute or so later, Bansi was gritting her teeth and holding on tight as the green Morris Minor Traveller roared out of the harbour car park. It cornered sharply, narrowly missing a couple of thankfully quite agile pedestrians, and turned towards Ballyfey.

None of the occupants noticed the swan, far above and matching their speed perfectly.

Nor did they notice the grey wolf that tracked them stealthily across country, keeping itself well hidden from view.

Chapter Four

Night was beginning to fall by the time they neared home. Fintan O'Hara was fast asleep in the back of the car, long legs folded uncomfortably behind the driver's seat, head slumped awkwardly against the window. Asha O'Hara, mirroring him, slumbered against the opposite window, her Asian good looks only slightly marred by the trickle of dribble oozing from her open, snoring mouth. Between them, Bansi was sleeping soundly, her dreams filled with the startlingly beautiful scenery of the day's drive.

'It's been a long old day for them, hasn't it?' Nora Mullarkey remarked.

'It has that, Nora,' her friend said. 'They'll have had to get up in the middle of the night to get to the ferry in— *Look out!*'

For the second time that day, the car screeched urgently to a halt. Its rear wheels skidded violently. The dark shape in the road turned; two yellow eyes stared at them malevolently, gleaming in the head-lights. Then it was gone.

The two old women looked at each other.

'What was *that*?' Eileen O'Hara asked shakily.

Nora Mullarkey looked grim. 'A wolf,' she said. 'Without a shadow of a doubt, that was a wolf in the road.'

Eileen O'Hara looked at her friend in amazement. She laughed nervously. 'Nora, talk sense! You know as well as I do that there've been no wolves in Ireland for hundreds of years.'

'Aye, well it was no ordinary wolf, was it? That'll have been one of the Good People.'

'The Good . . . Och, Nora, not your old stories about the fai—'

'Eileen!' Mrs Mullarkey's voice cracked like a whip. 'You will *not* be so foolish as to say the word! Not after what we've just seen!'

'Whatever that animal was, Nora, it was just an animal, and no more than that.'

'Oh aye? There are more things in heaven and on earth than are dreamt of in *your* philosophy, Eileen O'Hara, that's for sure!'

'Well, even if your old stories *were* true, what' – Granny paused sarcastically – 'would *they* be doing wandering around here in this day and age?'

In the back seat, Bansi stirred. Somewhere in her dreams, two unpleasant yellow eyes stared unblinkingly at her through a chilly grey mist.

The sound of her grandmother's voice came to her, as if calling her to a place of safety, and she turned. Her heavy-lidded eyes opened sleepily and she found herself in the car, gazing drowsily into the deepening twilight. Only half awake, she found herself looking at a great hill that rose above the lights of the distant village. It seemed to have a light of its own; a pale shimmer that hung around it like nothing she'd ever seen before.

'Granny,' she said sleepily, 'why's that hill glowing?'

The women looked at Bansi, and saw that she was staring blearily in the direction of Slieve Donnan – the great hill which stood to the east of the village. The hill on which the ancient stone circle lay. The hill from which, unknown to them, the wolf had come that morning.

A hill which, as far as they could see, was not glowing in the slightest.

'Don't you worry about that, young lady,' Mrs Mullarkey told her firmly. 'You just go on back to sleep. We're nearly there now.' She ground the car into first gear once more and moved off, uncharacteristically slowly.

Bansi's eyelids closed again and she felt the warm blanket of sleep settle itself around her. Comfortably, she drifted off.

Mrs Mullarkey leaned over the gear lever towards her friend.

'Maybe it's her,' she muttered. 'Maybe there's something of the Good People about your granddaughter.'

Eileen O'Hara looked as if she'd been slapped. 'Nora! What are you saying!'

'Oh, come on, Eileen! You heard what her mother said about the swan following her! And then one of the Good People appears before us in the guise of a wolf – and she sees a glow around Slieve Donnan, of all places! That's no coincidence! And on Midsummer's Eve, too!'

'So what? You're telling me she's a ... a *changeling*, is that it?'

'Or something of the sort. After what we've just seen, I'd bet my life on it.'

Granny looked at her friend calculatingly. 'Or your pension?'

'*What?*'

'Or your pension,' Granny repeated. 'I'll bet my week's pension against yours that you're wrong. You can do your old eggshell test tonight – I shan't breathe a word to her. The week's pension goes to the winner. Which,' she added confidently, 'will be me.'

Nora Mullarkey, grim-faced, glanced back at Bansi. 'You're on,' she said. With one final look back at Bansi, she shifted gears and stamped on the accelerator.

High above, a ghostly white shape shadowed the car soundlessly: an owl, drifting through the gathering twilight, unobserved from the ground.

The wolf briefly broke cover again, darting across the road and disappearing once more into the undergrowth. The owl watched without expression.

'Told you,' grumbled the little brown man who rode on its back. '*Now* will you listen, Tam? That's one of *them* down there, and one I don't want to tangle with either.'

The owl hooted softly. 'Stop fussing, Pogo. I can handle him easy enough. I don't reckon he's a real shape-changer – more like a skin-changer; some kind of selkie, maybe, only with wolves instead of seals. I've heard of such creatures, but I've never seen one before. Mind you, I still say it'd be easier to take the child ourselves.'

Pogo bristled. 'It'd be easier still to go home, and let the Dark Lord have the child and do what he wants with her,' he snapped. 'But we're not going to do that either. We're here to protect her, nothing else.'

'Ah, talk sense, Pogo . . .'

'Talk sense yourself! This is the prophesied child, Tam! If the Dark Lord captures her, that's the end – for you, for me, for all of us who value our freedom. And that's why we have to keep her safe – and keep her away from the Other Realm at all costs, for now at least. That's what was decided . . .'

'Aye, and I still say it was the wrong decision. Look, Pogo – no, hear me out,' Tam quickly added as Pogo drew breath to argue. 'The prophecy will be fulfilled. Sooner or later, the child *has* to stand on the sacred earth of Tir na n'Óg. Why not sooner?'

'Because she's just a child! And because now –

while the Dark Lord is looking for her – the risk is too great! The gate between this world and ours will only be open until tomorrow night. Once it's closed again, she'll be safe. For now, at least.'

'Aye, and we'll be trapped here. Maybe for decades. Pogo, you know that the gate only opens for a few days each year, and you know this is the first time she's ever been this close to it at one of those times. She could be an old woman before it happens again! If we don't take her back with us tonight – try to fulfil the prophecy ourselves, before the Dark Lord finds her – then we're stuck here. Do you really want that? Can you bear to live in this terrible place, with its air half poisoned by those car things, not knowing when you'll see your own home again? Is that what you're saying?'

'It was what *you* said, too!' Pogo snapped. 'Have you forgotten? You promised, as did I, in front of Caithne and all the others, to protect the girl until she was grown, and bring her to the Other Realm to fulfil the prophecy only when she was old enough to make that decision herself!'

'I promised, Pogo, because you wouldn't come with me unless I did. And without you, I'd never have found the child in time, and the Dark Lord would have seized her. But that doesn't mean I have to like it. I miss the Other Realm already. This mortal world – it's nothing compared to Tir na n'Óg . . .'

Pogo's face softened a little, and when he spoke again his tone was less harsh. 'It's a brave thing you're doing, Tam. A few years in the land of mortals isn't such a hardship for my kind as for yours. But it has to be this way . . . no, now it's *your* turn to hear *me* out, so listen. I know that for the prophecy to be fulfilled, this girl must come to the Other Realm – one day. But she's just a child. The Other Realm is no place for mortal children. Maybe when she's older, if you and I are able to prepare her for what she's likely to face there; maybe then we can ask her to come with us. But to take her now would be to put her in terrible danger and I won't do that.'

'Ah, we'd keep her safe, Pogo. And you've said it yourself – countless lives hang in the balance here. If the Dark Lord is the one who fulfils the prophecy, it'll be ruin for all of us. We have to stop him!'

'We *are* stopping him, you thickhead. If we keep the girl safe till the gate closes once more, he can't get to her.'

'Aye, and then we're trapped here; and maybe when the gate reopens he'll send someone else after her anyway. Or maybe that one down there in the wolfskin is under instructions to stay here and watch her if he can't get her straight away. There's so many maybes, Pogo; but if we take the girl now, and fulfil the prophecy ourselves before he can get to her, then he's lost and the Other Realm is saved.'

Pogo scowled. 'The decision's been made, Tam, and it's not ours to change. We agreed it with all the others, in case you'd forgotten. With me, you stood before Caithne and all her company, the whole fellowship of the Sacred Grove, and you promised.'

'Only because we needed you to find the girl, and you said you wouldn't do it unless we did it your way!'

'No! Because I said I wouldn't be party to kidnapping a child! And that still stands, whatever happens!' Pogo glared down at the top of the owl's head. 'We stick to the plan, Tam – however long it takes. We're here to protect her, not to steal her away. And when she goes back home across the sea, we go with her, and watch over her and try to prepare her for the future. All right?'

A change in movement, far below, caught Tam's eye. 'They're pulling up at a house.'

'Do you see the wolf?'

'No. He'll be somewhere around, I don't doubt.'

'Right, Tam. You stand guard outside. I'll go in and keep watch over the girl.'

'Hold on tight, then. Down we go!'

Like a silent white thunderbolt the owl dropped towards the earth, watched from the night shadows by two cold yellow eyes.

Chapter Five

All was quiet in Granny O'Hara's house; but as the grandfather clock in the hallway struck midnight, Bansi woke to the realization that somebody was in the bedroom with her. Two shadowy figures were moving around, murmuring to each other in voices softer than a whisper. Heart hammering, she peered through the slits of her eyelids. The intruders weren't burglars, as far as she could tell. They weren't taking anything from the room; rather, they seemed to be placing something – a number of somethings – around her bed. Nor – though it was difficult to tell in the darkness – did they look big or threatening. They certainly weren't the huge and fearsome men she'd always imagined burglars to be. They looked more like – well, two little old ladies, really. In fact, one of them looked very like – no, exactly like . . .

'Granny!' Bansi exclaimed in exasperation, sitting up and switching the light on. 'What *are* you doing? It's the middle of the night, and you and–' She peered at the other figure and groaned to herself. 'You and Mrs Mullarkey are creeping round me while I'm asleep! Is there a reason for this, or are you both just pretending to be completely bonkers?'

Granny blushed, and looked as if she might say something, but Mrs Mullarkey glared her into silence, raising one bony finger to her lips as she did so, and they both carried on with what they were doing. Bansi watched, intrigued in spite of herself.

While she was sleeping, the two women had begun to lay out around her a circle of twelve neatly hollowed-out eggshells, each one perched precariously on a makeshift cradle on top of a small gas camping stove. Each eggshell was half full of water and, as she watched, her grandmother and Mrs Mullarkey lit the flames. Then Mrs Mullarkey, standing ramrod straight, folded her arms and looked at her as if waiting for something.

Bansi waited, too. Shell by shell, the water began to bubble. Mrs Mullarkey continued to stare at her. Granny, meanwhile, leaned against the door and looked at Mrs Mullarkey. They waited . . . and waited . . . and waited . . . and finally, Bansi could wait no longer.

'OK,' she said. 'You're boiling water in eggshells, is that it?'

Mrs Mullarkey's eyebrows lifted expectantly, but she said nothing.

'So *is* that it?' Bansi persisted. 'Or is there more? Because I'm really tired and, Granny, I don't want to sound ungrateful if this is some kind of entertainment you put on for all your guests, but I would *really* like to go back to sleep now. Please?'

Mrs Mullarkey looked somehow disappointed. 'You're not going to tell me you've seen this before, I hope?' she asked.

'Of course not,' Bansi answered, perhaps a little too sharply.

'Aha!' said Mrs Mullarkey triumphantly.

'Why should I? There aren't any bonkers old ladies in my house back home. And I'm only ten. Maybe all the ten-year-olds round here are used to this, but in that case I'd really appreciate your going and giving them another look and letting me get back to sleep!' And then, feeling that perhaps she'd been a little rude, she added, 'Please?'

Mrs Mullarkey looked as if she'd popped a sweet into her wrinkled mouth and discovered it was broccoli-and-sawdust flavour.

But Granny clapped her hands and rubbed them together gleefully. 'There you are, Nora! Nothing of the changeling about my Bansi. I hope you won't miss next week's pension too much – I'll certainly be glad of the extra, I can tell you!'

Bansi was outraged. 'Granny!' she said angrily. 'You don't mean to tell me that you and Mrs Mullarkey woke me up in the middle of the night and boiled water in eggshells round my bed just for a *bet*, do you?'

Mrs Mullarkey and Granny looked at each other like two naughty children caught pulling each other's pigtails. Bansi half expected one of them to say, 'Well, she started it,' but neither of them did.

Instead, Mrs Mullarkey said, 'It's not *just* about a bet, young lady . . .'

'What *is* it about, then?' Bansi asked, and when neither of them answered she burst out, 'Oh, come on! You've woken me up; it'll take ages to get back to sleep now. I think the least you can do is tell me what it's all about!'

There was a pause.

'Oh, all right, then,' said Granny. 'I suppose you're right. It's got to do with some silly stories about the f— *Ow!*'

Mrs Mullarkey had pinched her, hard. 'You will *not* be so foolish as to say the word, Eileen O'Hara!'

'Well, how am I going to tell her if I can't tell her? Talk some sense!'

'Oh, be quiet. Bansi, what we're going to tell you has to do with the F-A-E-R-Y folk.'

Bansi spelled it out in her head. 'What,' she said, puzzled. 'Fairies?'

Behind the curtain, a small brown man winced, and shook his head.

High in the branches of a tree outside, the ghostly figure of an owl turned its head sharply.

And in the darkest corner of the garden, two glowing yellow eyes raised their cold unblinking stare, and seemed to look straight through the walls of the house into the room.

'Quiet, child!' Mrs Mullarkey hissed, gripping her walking stick so tightly that all her knuckles turned white. 'For goodness' sake – and I *mean* that, for the sake of all the goodness there is in this world – don't say that word!'

'Why not? What's wrong with f—'

'*Shut up*, girl!'

There was an awkward pause.

'Um . . . Mrs Mullarkey,' said Bansi hesitantly after a moment, 'I don't want to be rude or anything, but – well – there's no such thing as . . . I mean . . . you're not trying to tell me you're frightened of Tinkerbell, are you?'

Mrs Mullarkey gave a dry barking laugh. 'Tinkerbell, indeed. I wish, child. I wish that the Good People were all wee Tinkerbells. No – they're very real, and they're evil, the lot of them.'

Pogo glared out unseen from behind the curtain, and bared his little teeth at her.

Bansi wrinkled her forehead in puzzlement. 'Hang on – what do you mean, the good people are evil? That doesn't make sense.'

'These . . . beings we're talking of,' Mrs Mullarkey said impatiently. 'If you name them by one of their true names – if you call them what they really are – they will hear you. You don't want that, young Bansi. You don't want to come to their attention, believe you me, for they *are* evil – or at the very least, full of thoughtless mischief. They have uncanny powers. They can take on different shapes, and bewitch people and much else besides. And they use these powers for wickedness. That's why folk began to call them the Good People, for whatever else they may be, they're certainly not good.'

Bansi felt they'd got a little off the point. 'All right, Mrs Mullarkey – but what has this got to do with you and my granny creeping round my bed at midnight boiling water in eggshells?'

Mrs Mullarkey said nothing. She suddenly looked a little sheepish.

Bansi waited, patiently.

'Oh, for goodness'sake, Nora,' said Granny, kneeling to turn off the camping stoves. 'If you won't tell the child, I will.' She paused, but still Mrs Mullarkey said nothing. 'Very well,' Granny went on, turning to Bansi. 'What it is, sweetheart, is this: according to the old stories about the – the Good People, one of their tricks is to steal a human baby from its cradle and replace it with one of their own kind – a changeling. And Nora here thought that perhaps . . .'

'Thought that *I* might be a changeling?' Bansi almost laughed. 'And the eggshells help you find out?'

Mrs Mullarkey, not quite meeting Bansi's gaze, nodded. 'The surest way of telling a changeling from a human child is to let it see you boiling water or brewing beer or cooking a meal in hollowed-out eggshells. If the child really is one of the Good People, it'll say something like, "Six hundred years have I lived in the Land of Youth" – or Tir na n'Óg, or F-A-E-R-Y; it's all one and the same – "but never have I seen the likes of that!" '

'And then it flies up the chimney and vanishes away back home, or some such nonsense,' Granny added.

'And this works every time, does it?' Bansi asked.

'Without fail!' Mrs Mullarkey declared.

'So – are they really that stupid?' Bansi asked.

Mrs Mullarkey's eyebrows shot up like a couple of startled pheasants. 'What on earth do you mean, child?'

'Well – for one thing, if they've lived six hundred years in the land of whatever, wouldn't they be clever enough to know not to tell? Especially if every so often one of their changeling friends comes back home and says, "You won't *believe* what I've just done! Remember the eggshell trick? Oldest one in the book, and I just fell for it *again*" . . .'

Mrs Mullarkey pursed her lips. 'It's not a matter of *clever*, young lady,' she announced disapprovingly. 'It's *tradition*. Some things just happen because they're supposed to, and no amount of cleverness or knowing things can change them. So there! Like the use of iron. Who knows why they fear it, or why it cancels their magic? But they do, and it does, and there's an end to it!'

'Iron?'

The old woman nodded. 'It's the surest defence against them there is. All the old stories agree.'

'What about steel, then?' asked Bansi curiously, drawn in despite herself. 'Does that work, too?'

'Steel?' Mrs Mullarkey demanded stiffly. 'What on earth do you mean? It's *iron* that works against them.'

'Yes, but steel's made out of iron,' Bansi pointed out. 'We did it in science last term. So surely if iron works then steel should too?'

'Stuff and nonsense! Iron is iron, and it's only iron that'll keep you safe! Any more silly questions?'

'Well – yes, actually.' Bansi was beginning to enjoy herself. 'What about . . . um . . . B-R-O-W-N-I-E-S? They're "Good People" as well, aren't they? Are you telling me that they come and tidy your house as part of some evil plan?'

Mrs Mullarkey glared scornfully at Bansi. 'Brownies,' she said tersely, not noticing the sudden twitching from behind the curtain, 'are wee girls who come round selling biscuits. The creatures you're referring to don't exist, and never have. Little men coming at night to do your housework for you, indeed! As if any of the Good People would want to do a single thing to help mortal humans! In any case, how would they get in your house?'

'Um . . . through the door?' Bansi suggested.

Mrs Mullarkey shook her head disbelievingly. 'Do you know nothing, child? The Good People can't enter a human dwelling unless they're invited.'

Granny chuckled dryly. 'Well, they can come in my house, and welcome,' she said, 'along with the man in the moon and the Wizard of Oz. I could do with some help with the housework.'

Mrs Mullarkey turned in fury. 'Eileen O'Hara, of all the foolish things to say! You'd better just pray that none of *them* is listening! For they'll take that as an invitation, you can be sure! Now you'll need protection! What have you in the house that's made of iron?'

Eileen O'Hara rolled her eyes. 'If you must play your silly games, Nora, I've an old iron skillet above the stove in the kitchen and a poker by the fire. And thinking about it, now, there's a couple of boxes full of junk metal that's been in the garage about twenty years; if you'd like to take all of that, you'd be doing me a favour . . .'

'Right,' Mrs Mullarkey said. 'I'll start gathering all that together. You stay here and mind the child. And keep your silly old mouth shut, if you can!'

She swept dramatically out through the door.

Granny shook her head and looked at Bansi. 'Well,' she said, her eyes smiling merrily, 'now that you're awake, how would you like a very large omelette?'

And they both burst out laughing.

That was when the window exploded. Bansi whirled at the sound. She heard Granny scream, a long loud piercing sound. There was a torrent of broken glass; a great grey shape leaping at her.

It landed heavily, bearing her to the ground. She felt hot savage breath on her neck as sharp animal teeth closed on her throat.

Chapter Six

Bansi was paralysed, her limbs heavy and useless. She could hear Granny's voice screaming and cursing at the beast, and the sound of two elderly fists pounding uselessly on the broad grey back, but she could see nothing except one cruel yellow eye set hard in velvet fur, staring into hers. Then the pressure eased on her throat and she gasped as the wolf released its hold.

It locked eyes with her again for a moment, its hot carnivorous breath almost suffocating her, before its head snapped round to turn its evil gaze on her grandmother. Bansi could see the muscles under its coat ripple with treacherous, fluid strength as it curved smoothly away from her, slinking round threateningly to face the old woman.

She wanted to cry out – to tell her granny to run – but her voice, as if enchanted, refused to obey her. The wolf growled softly, its savage teeth exposed in a vicious snarl. From where Bansi lay she could see Granny's face, at once furious and fearful. She tried to move, but her body would not respond. The wolf tensed to spring.

Behind Granny, the bedroom door burst open. Bansi saw Mrs Mullarkey framed in the doorway, brandishing a cast-iron skillet. The wolf pounced; the old woman stepped forward and swung. There was a satisfying *thud* as the pan connected, and the wolf fell to the floor with a surprised expression on its suddenly unconscious face.

Then Granny was kneeling over her, anxious and concerned. 'Are you hurt, sweetheart?'

Bansi tried to answer, but she could do no more than move her eyes. Even speech was beyond her. She felt numb all over, and uncomfortably drowsy. She looked into her granny's worried face; heard her say, 'Nora! There's something wrong with Bansi!'

Mrs Mullarkey shouldered her granny out of the way. 'Did it hurt you, girl?'

Again Bansi tried to answer, but her voice was paralysed and useless. The world began to swim around her, odd colours appearing in a blur at the edge of her vision. She heard her grandmother's voice, echoing strangely and distantly.

'It had her by the throat. But there's no blood.'

She felt herself slipping away now, as if some mysterious other realm had reached out to her and was drawing her into it.

Mrs Mullarkey's voice murmured at the edge of her consciousness, 'It'll be some magic, I don't doubt. Maybe the touch of iron will do it.'

There was a sharp tingling, an icy shock. Bansi felt her senses gasp; her nerves fired, shocked and alert. As if thrown into a cold pool on a hot drowsy day, her body flung off the enchanted lethargy. Her eyes snapped open; she found herself staring at Mrs Mullarkey, who was gently but firmly holding the edge of the iron skillet against her neck, just where the wolf's teeth had gripped her.

A subtle warmth began to flow through Bansi; her throat throbbed, as if the iron was drawing out some strange poison from the wolf's bite. She blinked; moved her head; tried to speak.

'Whoa,' she muttered. Tentatively, she flexed her

fingers; moved her arms; eased herself upright. 'That was weird. And not in a good way.'

Granny hugged her, held her tight. 'Are you all right, love?' she asked.

Bansi's head spun for a second; she blinked. Mrs Mullarkey held the skillet out to her, handle-first. Reflexively, she gripped it tight and the numbness and pain fell away from her like autumn leaves. In an instant she was clear-headed again. 'I think so . . . Yes, yes I am, I'm fine,' she said, puzzled, staring at the shattered window, and the huge, shaggy creature which lay, unmoving, where the blow from the skillet had felled it. 'What's going on? That's – is that a *wolf*? But it can't be . . .' She looked at Mrs Mullarkey, who returned her gaze unblinkingly. 'You're going to say, "I told you so", aren't you?'

The old woman said nothing for a moment, but a small victorious smile tugged at her lips. 'Well, I did, didn't I?' she said after a moment. 'Maybe now some-one else'll admit to the truth of what I've been saying all these years – eh, Eileen?' she added, glancing at her friend triumphantly.

'You think this is one of . . . them, then?' Bansi asked, a little more respectfully. 'But what's it doing here?'

'That, young Bansi,' Mrs Mullarkey said grimly, 'is what we need to find out.'

'Would the eggshells be any use, do you think?' Granny asked.

'Talk some sense, would you, Eileen! The eggshells are for revealing changelings. We already know this creature is one of the Good People.'

'I'm only doing my best, Nora! I'm sorry if that's not good enough for you. I just thought that since you don't seem to have any ideas yourself, you might need some help, that's all.'

'Some *help* would be greatly appreciated, Eileen. What's not so welcome is silly ideas from someone who knows nothing about what we're dealing with here because she's spent her whole life scoffing.'

'Well! It just seemed to me that if you, Nora Maura Margaret Mullarkey, being our resident *expert* on fai— on the Good People, weren't coming up with the goods, I might be able to contribute something – but if that's not the case, I'll go and start the water boiling.'

'Eileen! Will you stop being so stubborn! I've just *told* you; boiling water in eggshells is no use for this.'

Granny cut her friend short with a withering stare. 'Eggshells? Who said anything about eggshells? *I'm* going to make a cup of tea!'

She flounced expertly out of the room.

Nora Mullarkey shook her head. 'Bansi,' she said,

'go and get that poker your granny was talking about. Then see what else you can find in the house that might be made of iron. We may need all the protection we can get.'

Bansi nodded, eager to be doing something. 'OK. I'll go and look through those boxes of junk in the garage, too.'

'No!' the old woman said sharply. She took the frying pan from Bansi and pointed at the wolf, still prone on the floor. 'That one there might have some friends with him. It's not safe to leave the house. Don't even go in the cellar until you've armed yourself – just in case. With iron, mind!' she added, her voice severe. 'None of your steel nonsense!'

Bansi caught the sense of urgency behind the old woman's harsh tone. She closed the door behind her and hurried off on her errand, head swimming with the events of the last few minutes.

Gripping her makeshift weapon, Mrs Mullarkey went carefully to the shattered window and looked out. There was no sign of movement. She turned back again – and froze in surprise. Where the unconscious wolf had lain just a moment before, there now sat, cross-legged on the floor, a cruel-faced boy dressed in animal skins. Beside him lay a shaggy pelt, as if someone had dumped an old rug there.

Mrs Mullarkey raised the skillet, gripping its

smooth handle tightly, and stepped forward. 'That'll be your skin on the floor there, will it?' she enquired. 'I hope you know a good glazier. That's an awful lot of damage you've done to my friend's window.'

The boy smiled. It wasn't a pleasant smile. 'Get rid of the frying pan, old woman,' he said. 'You're going to help me, not hit me.'

'*Help* you? I think you've got that wrong, young fellow-me-wolf. You're going to tell me who you are and what you want with my friend's granddaughter. Or I *will* hit you again, and you won't wake up so quickly this time, I'll promise you that.'

The boy laughed. The laugh was even less pleasant than the smile. 'If it's a name you want, you can call me Conn. It's not my real name, of course – but then it can be dangerous giving a stranger your name, can't it, Nora Maura Margaret Mullarkey?'

Mrs Mullarkey stopped, confused. She blinked, and threw the pan out of the window. 'Sorry,' she said, 'what did you say?'

'You're going to go downstairs now and tell your friend that I escaped, but that it isn't important. Say whatever it takes to put her mind at rest. As soon as you can, and however you have to, get her out of the way. *However* you have to,' he repeated malevolently. 'And when I return before dawn's first light – you're going to hand the girl over to me.'

Mrs Mullarkey nodded. 'If it'll help, young man, I'm always happy to oblige.'

'Nora!' Eileen O'Hara said, surprised, as the kitchen door opened. 'You haven't left Bansi guarding that creature, have you?'

What creature . . . ?' said Nora Mullarkey. 'Oh – oh, *him*. No, he got away. Now, how about that cup of tea?'

'Got away?' Mrs O'Hara's mouth fell open in surprise. 'Well – shouldn't we call the police or something?'

'Och, no, Eileen, why would we want to make such a fuss as that? I'm sure he's perfectly harmless!'

'Nora, he's a *wolf*!'

'Ach, well, we're none of us perfect, are we? Now, what about that tea?'

Granny stood obstinately, furiously still. 'Nora Maura Margaret Mullarkey, what is *wrong* with you?' she spluttered.

Mrs Mullarkey pushed past her. 'If you're not going to make it, Eileen, I'm sure you won't mind if I help myself. Some of us are thirsty, you know.'

Upstairs, Pogo peeked warily from his hiding place as Conn swept the wolfskin cloak over his shoulders and drew the fur together at the throat, where by some magic it joined seamlessly. He watched the boy pull the grisly hood over his head and draw the cloak around him. He saw the garment wrap itself around the boy, clinging and bonding; watched the muscles thicken, rippling beneath the pelt, as the great beast leaped without effort through the shattered window and disappeared into the darkness below.

Face grim, the little man turned and looked around the room. It was littered with shards of glass and pieces of broken window frame; there were matted tufts of wolf-fur on the furniture, and muddy paw prints on the floor. The bedside rug had been kicked into a heap during the scuffle and several of the camping stoves had been knocked over, spilling the water and scattering fragments of eggshell everywhere. Besides which, he noticed, Granny hadn't been too careful about dusting lately – and as for the state of the carpet under the bed . . .

Pogo felt himself gripped by an uncontrollable urge – a primeval impulse, stronger than his sense of duty; stronger almost than his survival instinct. It was irresistible.

Somewhere in the back of his mind, his conscience whispered to him: *Ignore it! Find Tam! Keep the girl safe!*

Yes, yes, another voice in his head replied impatiently, *but this'll only take a minute.*

We may not have *a minute!* his conscience reminded him frantically. *There's a powerful enemy on the loose! He's bewitched the old woman! He's going to take the child!*

Aye, there is that, the other voice answered. *But that said . . . I mean . . .* look *at this mess! I'm a brownie, for goodness sake! I can't just go off saving people when there's housework to be done!*

But . . . but . . . well, yes, it is a bit of a tip, his conscience conceded. *And it won't take* very *long, will it?*

No, not long at all, the other voice soothed. *Look – we'll get started now, shall we?*

Pogo, thoroughly under the spell of his own instincts, began to gather the broken glass together. A brush would have helped, but his hands were tough and he knew what he was doing. Within seconds, he was lost in concentration.

Until, that is, the spell was broken by the firm press of a cold point of iron against the back of his neck.

'Turn round very slowly,' Bansi O'Hara said. 'And no funny business.'

Pogo turned round and looked up at the girl who stood over him, an ornate poker held sword-like and threatening in her hand.

Bansi glared down at the small intruder, filled with anger and apprehension. She had no idea how dangerous the little man might be, though at least he seemed to have fewer teeth than the wolf. 'And you would be . . . ?' she asked, trying to hold her voice steady.

The little man glowered. 'I would be . . . very much obliged if you'd stop waving that thing about, that's what I would be,' he said. 'Anyway, it doesn't work on me,' he added, grabbing the end of the poker suddenly, twisting it out of her hands and shaking it aggressively in her face.

Bansi stepped back warily, eyes casting around for another weapon. 'Hang on,' she said. 'You do know that's made of iron, don't you?'

'Oh, is it?' sneered the manikin, moving towards her, poker still raised. 'Well, that doesn't affect me, does it? Because apparently I don't exist. I'm just a wee girl who comes round selling biscuits. Which means I could knock your brains out with this if I wanted to!' He lifted the poker as if to strike, baring his teeth in a dreadful scowl, and threw it over his shoulder. It struck the wall by the shattered window with a dull clanging sound. 'So now we've established that,' he said, 'perhaps you'll believe me when I tell you I'm here to help.' With one agile movement, he leaped onto the bed and looked her in the eye.

Bansi regarded him suspiciously. 'Why should I trust you?' she asked. 'You're one of the "Good People", aren't you? Like that wolf. In fact, how do I know you're *not* the wolf, in another disguise?'

The little man's leathery face creased into a deep frown. 'For goodness' sake, girl! I'm a brownie! We don't do all that changing shape nonsense! We're *nice* faeries, all right?'

'According to Mrs Mullarkey, there aren't any nice . . . what you said,' Bansi pointed out.

'Aye, well according to that silly old fool, there aren't any brownies at all. But here I am.'

'And how do I know you're really a brownie?'

Pogo lifted his hands skywards in exasperation. 'Look at me! I'm a wee brown man in a brown loincloth! You've just caught me tidying up! What *else* would I be? Besides which, like I said, iron doesn't affect me – look.' Leaping off the bed, he picked up the poker in one hand and slapped it against the other. 'See? We couldn't have tidied up around you big gallumphers if we couldn't touch your iron pots and pans, now, could we? Come to that, we don't have to wait to be invited in, which is how come I was able to see those old biddies doing all the non-sense with the eggshells. So there you go, I'm a brownie, and if you don't mind I'd quite like to save your life. If it's all the same to you.'

'Save my life? That's a bit over the top, isn't it?'

The little man bounded back onto the bed and drew his face close to Bansi's.

'Over the top?' he said. 'Not at all. That wolf is a shape assumed by Conn, a faery warrior of the Dark Sidhe. He is here to kidnap you, and to take you back to the Other Realm – the Land of Faery. Me? I'm Pogo. I've been sent to protect you. And believe me when I say that right now, I'm just about the only thing standing between you and certain death.'

Chapter Seven

Bansi felt laughter welling up inside her. The idea of this little man as some kind of hero sent to save her was ridiculous. In fact, the whole situation was ridiculous. None of it could possibly be true.

Except that a wolf *had* attacked her. And there *was* a brownie in her room. Suddenly she found she was simultaneously trembling and wanting to giggle uncontrollably. Taking a deep breath, she sat down hard on the bed, clenching her fists in order to steady herself.

'Sorry,' she said. 'But there must be some kind of mistake. I mean, I don't even . . . *didn't* even believe in f— in, um, you people. And I've never heard of this "Dark She" woman–'

Impatiently, the little man cut her off. 'It's not "she" like a woman. It's S-I-D-H-E, "Shee". The sidhe are one of the oldest faery races–'

'Hang on,' Bansi broke in suspiciously. 'Should you be using that word?'

'A mortal shouldn't, but it's safe enough for a

faery,' Pogo retorted. 'And us brownies are faery beings, whatever that old battleaxe friend of your granny's may tell you. As are the sidhe, which brings me back to what I was saying: the Court of the Dark Sidhe is one of the faery kingdoms, and it's the Lord of the Dark Sidhe–'

Already Bansi was having difficulty keeping up. 'Is he the King of the . . . Good People?'

The brownie shook his head in scornful exasperation. 'Not at all. The Dark Lord is king of nothing but a bunch of hooligans and hoodlums. Ach, I suppose the Court of the Dark Sidhe is a kingdom, strictly speaking, but a very minor one; and if you ask me it's nothing but a gang of villains who've pledged allegiance to a bigger villain.'

'So the sidhe are the bad fai . . . what you said?'

This was met with a contemptuous roll of the eyes. 'There are good sidhe, bad sidhe and sidhe who just mind their own business. Same as mortals. Some of the worst of the faery folk are sidhe, I suppose – like the Dark Lord himself – but then so are some of the best and most noble. Most of the so-called Dark Sidhe aren't even of the sidhe race; they've just taken the name to make themselves sound better than they are. Look, do you really need the whole story now?'

Bansi was losing patience herself. 'Well, *some* kind of explanation would be nice. If there's someone trying to kill me, I'd like to know why. What's this Dark Lord got against me? And what brings you into all this?'

The little man tutted with irritation. 'Right. From the beginning, then.

'There are dozens of different faery races: the brownies, the sidhe, the púca, the blue men, the leprechaun, the cluricaun, the boggarts, the selkie, the merrows, the hags, the kelpie – to name but a few. The sidhe are the one of the oldest and most distinguished, most powerful and most magical. With me so far?' he added, with what Bansi felt was quite unnecessary sarcasm.

She nodded.

'Fine,' he went on. 'Now, some of the faery races tend towards the solitary, but some like to group together in tribes, or clans, or kingdoms, or fiefdoms. Like the Court of the Dark Sidhe. Whose Lord is the nasty piece of wickedness who sent that skin-changing wolf-fellow to get you.

'You see, the Lord of the Dark Sidhe discovered that you were for the first time in your life coming within reach of the gate, and on Midsummer's Eve, too – one of the very few days of the year when the gate opens. The wise and venerated Caithne of the Sacred Grove—'

'Hold on!' Bansi felt as if she was in danger of

being washed away on a flood of information, none of which she could make any sense of. But the idea was beginning to sink in that this really was about her, Bansi O'Hara; that she hadn't just been drawn into this strange world of wolf warriors and brownies and Dark Lords by chance; and somehow this scared her more than anything else. 'What gate? And what's so special about me?'

Pogo scowled darkly. 'If you wouldn't keep interrupting with your questions, perhaps you'd find out some of the answers!' he snapped. 'And if you knew enough of the old tales of your father's people, you'd know that once there were many ways and paths and routes between our world and yours. Many's a time some careless mortal would wander by accident into the Other Realm, not even knowing that they'd done so. But now only one way remains – the sole gateway between the realm of mortals and the land of Faery. In your world it stands not far from here, marked with an ancient circle of standing stones; in ours it may be entered from almost anywhere, but only by those few who have the power to do so. Most of the time it remains closed, and passage between our worlds is impossible. But at certain times of the year, it opens – in those magical few days when the barrier between the world of mortals and the world of Faery grows thinner. Even then, though, you can pass through it nowadays only during the twilight hours of dawn and dusk.

'As for what makes you so special: listen, and I'll come to that. But each thing in its turn.

'Now Caithne of the Sacred Grove learned that you were soon to come within reach of the gate; and she discovered that the Dark Lord knew this also. So as quick as she could she gathered together a fellowship – a company of faery folk who had no love for the Dark Sidhe or their Lord, and we held a council to decide what was to be done. All were agreed that it would bring great peril to our land were the Dark Lord to capture you, but there was much debate about how to stop him.

'Eventually it was decided to send two of us through the gate to find you and keep you safe. It was obvious who should go. Brownies have a deep instinctive understanding of the ways of mortals, almost a sixth sense, so I was chosen to find you, to watch over you and to do what I could to protect you. The other chosen was Tam, a púca who—'

'Sorry, but what's a púca?' The brownie's manner was beginning to grate on Bansi's frayed nerves; he seemed to assume she knew – or should know – all manner of things about the faery realm.

Pogo rolled his eyes impatiently. 'Do you know *none* of the old stories? A púca is another of the creatures of faery, one of the most magical. Many of the tales have them taking the form of a goat and causing mischief, but there's more to the púca than that – a lot more. Tam was the only one among us with the power to enter the gate when it opened. Besides, like all his kind, he's a shape-changer, which made him useful when we were tracking you.'

A tingle ran over Bansi's skin. She felt her heart kick, a little jerk of sudden realization. 'The swan! The swan that followed us? Was that him – this púca – in another shape?'

Pogo nodded. 'It was, aye; and me with him. Finding you and watching over you, as we were charged. And I'm sorry we haven't done a better job so far; Tam should have been able to stop any of the Dark Sidhe from reaching you.'

Bansi breathed deeply once more, and ran her fingers distractedly through her hair. For a moment, the thought flashed through her head that perhaps this was all a dream; that perhaps her grandmother and Mrs Mullarkey had never woken her up with their boiling of water in eggshells and their mad talk of changelings and faeries. Then she looked once more at the little brown man, and at the shattered window, and became aware of the chill night breeze through her thin pyjamas, and the thought evaporated. This had none of the qualities of a dream. It was real, however bizarre and unbelievable it felt, and what Pogo was telling her had to be the truth – unless he was somehow in league with the wolf. She shuddered, and pushed the idea from her mind.

'So you and this Tam are the good guys, and you're here to stop the bad guys getting me. But I still don't get why any of you should be interested in me in the first place.' She looked enquiringly at the brownie, feeling suddenly tired and confused, and desperately wanting to understand.

'I suppose I must tell you,' Pogo sighed, 'although we don't really have time for this. It has to do with a history of betrayal and death, and with an ancient prophecy – a prophecy that points to you, young lady,' he added, looking her in the eye so suddenly and intensely that Bansi's heart twisted inside her. 'I don't suppose you know any of the ancient stories – the Irish fairy tales, you'd call them?'

Bansi shook her head.

'Typical mortal,' Pogo muttered sourly. 'No idea who she is or where she comes from. All right, then: imagine a world that exists alongside your own. One where all kinds of beings dwell – little people, beautiful elves, hideous monsters.

'Now imagine that these creatures can walk into your world, and you into theirs, as easy as you can stroll across the garden. This was the Other Realm, long, long ago, in the days of the old tales. And in those days, the power of Faery was much greater, much stronger than it is now. There were some who could create a storm that would reduce a city to dust, or turn an entire army of warriors into sparrows. But not any more; and in a moment I'll tell you why.

'The Other Realm – the land of Faery, Tir na n'Óg, call it what you will – has always been a vast country of tribes, clans and alliances, of small kingdoms and of solitary dwellers who live under no one's rule or law. Over one of these kingdoms – the greatest of the kingdoms of Tir na n'Óg, though it was still small by your standards – ruled a king named Derga, a faery of the sidhe race.'

'But not one of the Dark Sidhe?' Bansi guessed.

Pogo nodded. 'In those days, there was no Court of the Dark Sidhe. And had there been, it wouldn't have stood a chance against the kingdom of Derga. No, he was one of the noblest sidhe who ever lived – a mighty warrior, too, and a great user of magic. He had two children, a daughter and a son whose names were Caer and Avalloc – these, at least, were the names they were commonly known by; no faery will ever reveal their true name if they can help it.'

'Why not?' Bansi wanted to know, puzzled.

'Because it gives others power over you, of course.

Now hold your whisht, and listen. We may not have much time.

'Caer and Avalloc were rare and gifted, even amongst the faery folk, and the people of their kingdom loved them. Not just of their own kingdom, either; their fame spread far and wide, and it began to be said that if ever the land of Faery were to be united, it would be under the rule of Caer and her brother Avalloc. They were known as the Morning Stars of Tir na n'Óg, for it was said that their reign would be the morning of a new day for the land of Tir na n'Óg, beside which all that had gone before would seem as dark as night. Some even said that the land itself, the very earth of the Other Realm, held them in the highest regard.

'But not everyone loved Caer and Avalloc. Amongst the rulers of the other kingdoms there were many who were jealous of them, and who began to plot against their lives, hoping with their own strong magic to seize control of the whole land of Faery once the Morning Stars were gone. And so it was that—'

'Excuse me,' Bansi broke in impatiently, 'but didn't you just say we didn't have much time? I don't mean to be rude, but I don't see what any of this has to do with a wolf trying to kill me.'

'Oh, it has everything to do with it,' Pogo assured her. 'Everything. You see, the plotters were very nearly successful. With cunning and magic, they turned the people against the Morning Stars: they murdered Derga, royal father to Caer and Avalloc, and made it appear as if his own children were the guilty ones.

'Caer and Avalloc had no choice but to flee the realm for the world of mortals. In those days, of course, the ways and paths between your world and ours were many; oftentimes a mortal could find himself in the Other Realm quite by accident. To the Morning Stars of Tir na n'Óg, it would have been as nothing to simply turn and step from the land of Faery into the world of humankind.

'But their enemies had worked strong magic against them, and they were separated as they fled. Caer found herself here, in Ireland, near to this very place. She came in mortal disguise to the court of the King of Donegal, and was welcomed. For her beauty, her wisdom, and her great courage and skill in battle, the king's son fell in love with her, and she became his princess and later his queen, bearing him a fine son within the year.

'Avalloc, meanwhile, found himself deep in the ancient forests of India. He dwelt there, suffering no harm from the animals and gaining a great reputation as a healer. In time he, too, married a mortal and fathered a child – a daughter, half-mortal and half-faery, like the child of Caer.

'But in the Other Realm their enemies still feared them, and feared their return. The enchantments they had used to turn the people against the Morning Stars were beginning to weaken.

'So by dark magic, cunning and treachery, they killed them.

'The night the Morning Stars were murdered, a fierce storm raged across the Other Realm and a great winter fell, as if the land itself were mourning the dead. And the power of Faery began to wane and dwindle. It was as if, in killing Caer and Avalloc, their enemies had somehow mortally wounded the very spirit of Tir na n'Óg. And the ways and paths and gateways between your world and ours began to close up and fade away, until only the gate on nearby Slieve Donnan – the hill that overlooks this very village – remained, marked by its ancient stone circle.

Even then the power faded, until now it's rare indeed that the gateway can be used: only on the most magical days of the year, in the twilit hours of dawn and dusk.'

Bansi was beginning to feel restless. She glanced at the ruined window, remembering uneasily how the wolf had burst through it. 'I still don't see what this has to do with me,' she said.

'You will. Caer and Avalloc were dead, but their children still lived. And those children grew up, and had children who grew up and had children, and so the bloodlines of the Morning Stars of Tir na n'Óg lived on.'

Light began to dawn in Bansi's mind. 'So – are you saying that I'm descended from one of them – from Caer, or from Avalloc? Is that what this is about? It's Caer, isn't it? Granny always says we're descended from the High Kings of Donegal . . .'

Pogo shook his little hairy head, and looked gravely into her eyes. 'Thousands of children, this mortal world over, are descended from one of the Morning Stars of Tir na n'Óg. That would be nothing special.

'But you, Bansi – you're different. For you are descended from both – from Caer through your father's line, and from Avalloc through your mother's. You are the first child in whom the bloodlines of Caer and Avalloc are reunited.'

In the sudden silence, Bansi felt the little man's gaze burning into her. 'But . . . I mean . . . the Dark Lord doesn't think I'm going to want to – I don't know . . .' She tailed off. The very idea seemed absurd; she could hardly bring herself to voice it. 'I mean . . . well . . . it's not like I'm going to want to – to become Queen of the Other Realm, or something, is it? Even if . . . I mean, just because my ancestors years ago might have been–'

Pogo cut her short. 'It's not just because of who your ancestors were, girl. It's because of what that makes you. It's because of the prophecy.'

His eyes took on a faraway look that made Bansi shiver – though with nervousness or excitement she wasn't sure. Intrigued, she felt herself being drawn in by the little brownie's story; and despite his gruff manner, something in her spirit believed him instinctively and wholeheartedly.

'For centuries,' Pogo went on, 'every faery of every race from the highest sidhe to the humble brownie has known this prophecy:

'When the Blood of the Morning Stars, joined and flowing together at last, is returned to the sacred earth as the light dies, then shall the power of Tir na n'Óg awaken. Then shall the ways between the worlds reopen. And the one who returns the blood to the land shall come into the inheritance of Derga.

'This prophecy, Bansi, points to you. You're the child with the Blood of the Morning Stars – the blood of Caer and of Avalloc – joined and flowing together through your veins. And when you return it to the sacred earth – when you come and stand in one of the three hundred and sixty-six sacred places of Tir na n'Óg – then–'

Bansi reacted as the implications of what Pogo was saying hit her. 'Hold on a moment! You're telling me you want me to go and just stand around somewhere in a land full of pixies and monsters so someone else can inherit something? Sorry – no way.' She looked at him with a fiercely felt defiance, daring him to argue.

But Pogo was nodding in agreement. 'I'm not asking you to do that. I'd not have agreed to bring you to Tir na n'Óg even if you'd asked me yourself. Not yet, anyway – not till you're old enough to deal with the dangers you might face there. And not even then,' he added as Bansi opened her mouth to protest, 'unless you agree to come. No, I was sent here to protect you – to stop someone else taking you.

'Because the Lord of the Dark Sidhe knows you are here, at last within reach of the only gateway left between your world and ours.'

A chill crept up Bansi's spine. 'And he wants this inheritance . . .'

'The inheritance of Derga. That's right. No one's entirely sure what the inheritance of Derga will be; some think it means his kingdom, which was conquered and broken up and shared out among the kingdoms of those who killed him. Some argue that, since Derga's children were likely to unite our realm, to become his heir is to become ruler of all Tir na n'Óg. Still others point to Derga's great magic and power, and claim that Derga's heir will become the most powerful enchanter in all the land. But whatever the inheritance of Derga may be, it will be something to be prized. So yes, the Dark Lord wants it. And believe me, he's not someone you want coming after you.'

Bansi swallowed. 'But he *is* coming after me.'

Pogo nodded grimly. 'Aye. And he'll do all he can to kidnap you, and use you to fulfil the prophecy and claim the inheritance of Derga. But for now at least, he only has until the sun sets tonight. You'll be safe enough after that.'

'Why? What happens tonight?'

The little man scowled again. 'Full of questions, aren't you?'

It was true; Bansi felt as if she could burst with all the things she wanted to know – not just for curiosity's sake, but because she felt that the more she knew, the more she could do. And there was still a small part of her that wondered if the brownie might be lying, and whether she could trip him up on some inconsistency. She held his gaze and waited for an answer.

The brownie sighed theatrically. 'You remember I said the gate would open only at certain magical times of the year? Midsummer is one of the most magical of all – a time when the veil that separates our two worlds is at its thinnest and most fragile. And so, in the twilight of dawn on the morning of Midsummer's Eve – almost a full day ago, now – the gate opened; and it will remain open until dusk has faded on Midsummer Day. Even so, the power of Faery is now so weak that the gate can only be passed through in the twilight times of dawn or dusk.' He paused, and fixed his bright old eyes upon her. 'Now you're going to ask me, "Why only at the twilight times?", aren't you? It's like this, girl: the magical times are the meeting times, the border times, the points of balance. Midsummer like midwinter, its mirror image, marks the moment when the lengthening days end and the lengthening nights begin; the meeting place between darkness and light, the place where the balance shifts. Dawn and dusk are the times when day meets night and neither has rule over the other. At those times, our worlds touch. That's why the gate opens at Midsummer, and why any may pass through it in the twilight times. And that is why the forces of the Dark Lord will try to take you to the stone circle, by this morning's dawn if they can, or by this evening's dusk. And why Tam and I will do all we can to keep the Dark Sidhe away from you – at all times, but especially before the day ends.'

He looked at Bansi with an expression so sincere that she almost felt reassured. With an effort, she forced a smile. 'Anyway,' she said, 'even if he does get me, he's just going to want to take me to one of your sacred places. I mean,' she added, seeing Pogo's expression darken once more, 'I know it'll be bad for you if he gets the inheritance, but he'll only want to take me to one of the sacred places and get me to stand there, won't he?'

Her heart sank, as Pogo's face took on an even more sombre look. 'Aye,' he said. 'Well. Now. It's like this. The thing is, you see, the Dark Lord has a different interpretation of the prophecy. Terrible literal, your sidhe, when the fancy takes them – especially the bad ones. No, he doesn't reckon that merely bringing you to one of the sacred places will be enough.

'The prophecy talks of the Blood of the Morning Stars, joined and flowing together, being returned to the sacred earth as the light dies. And everyone agrees that means the bearer of the bloodlines of the

Morning Stars – that's you – must stand in one of the sacred places of Tir na n'Óg as the sun sets. That's it – all you have to do is stand there.

'But the Lord of the Dark Sidhe sees it differently. He believes the prophecy means that the blood must actually flow into the sacred earth.'

Bansi felt her veins chill as she realized what Pogo was telling her. She wanted to cover her ears, to pretend she was asleep and dreaming and none of this was happening – anything but go on listening. Yet listen she did. The little man leaned forward, staring into her eyes with a blazing intensity.

'As far as the Dark Lord is concerned, to claim the inheritance of Derga, he must take you to one of the sacred places of Tir na n'Óg, and spill out your blood in sacrifice.

'Every last drop.'

Chapter Eight

Downstairs, Granny and Mrs Mullarkey were in the middle of a furious argument. Or at least Granny was; Mrs Mullarkey was being unusually, indeed worryingly, placid.

'Eileen,' she was saying, 'I keep telling you, there's nothing to worry about.'

'Nothing to worry about!' Granny almost shrieked. 'Nora, my window upstairs is in ruins because a big wolf jumped through it and attacked my granddaughter! And then it got away! And according to you that wolf is one of your blessed Good People in disguise!'

'Good People?' Nora Mullarkey asked teasingly. 'Come on, now, Eileen, aren't you getting a bit old to believe in fairies?'

Granny stared. In all the time she had known Nora Mullarkey – more than sixty years now – she had never once known her to say that word. Never. Something, she suddenly realized, was dreadfully wrong.

Her hand went to her mouth. 'Bansi!' she said, horrified. 'Where is she?'

'Oh, she's probably gone back to bed. She's tired, poor wee thing. Don't disturb her, Eileen. Sit down and drink your tea before it gets cold, why don't you?'

Granny ignored her, slamming the kitchen door on her way out.

Mrs Mullarkey shrugged, got calmly to her feet, opened one of the drawers and began to search.

At the top of the stairs, Eileen O'Hara paused. She could hear voices coming from Bansi's room.

One was definitely her granddaughter's; the other had a tone that was at once child-like and elderly.

As stealthily as she could, she moved along the landing and peered in. What she saw took her so much by surprise that she quite forgot herself.

'Heavens!' she burst out. 'A talking monkey!'

Bansi started guiltily, feeling somehow as if she'd been caught doing something wrong, while Pogo – in rather a wasted effort – drew himself up to his full height, and glared. 'If there's anyone in this room related to the monkeys,' he said coldly, 'she wasn't here a moment ago.'

Granny pulled herself together. 'Well,' she said, 'so what might you be?'

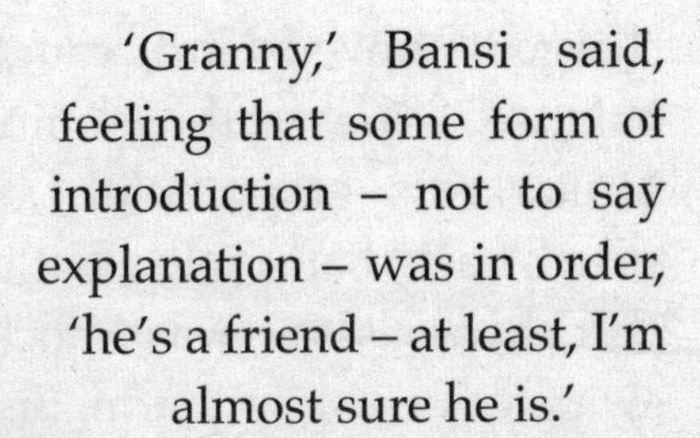

'Granny,' Bansi said, feeling that some form of introduction – not to say explanation – was in order, 'he's a friend – at least, I'm almost sure he is.'

'Oh, aye? What kind of a friend?' Granny sounded rather suspicious, Bansi thought.

'This is Pogo. He's a brownie.'

'A brownie, eh?' Granny asked, even more suspiciously, though her eyes flicked around the room and noticed the beginnings of the tidying up. 'Not here to get his bewitching badge, I hope. So, Mr Pogo, what can we do for you?'

Pogo harrumphed. 'It's more what I can do for you – or at least for the wee girl here . . .' he began.

A movement in the doorway caught Bansi's eye. She had no time to tell what it was, but all her senses were primed now for danger. 'Granny!' she shouted urgently. 'Look out!' She leaped off the bed.

Granny twisted round, and behind her Bansi saw Mrs Mullarkey, her face blank and expressionless, swing at her friend's head with a solid wooden rolling pin. Without thinking, Bansi acted: she charged; shoved hard; caught the old woman off-balance. The rolling pin slipped from Mrs Mullarkey's grasp. With surprising strength she struck back; Bansi felt a hot bruising pain across her cheekbone as she was knocked to the floor with a swipe of one skinny arm. She reached for the fallen rolling pin and grabbed it, but instantly Mrs Mullarkey's bony fingers closed on her hand and prised it from her, to turn once more on Granny O'Hara. Bansi picked herself up, threw herself desperately at the old woman, grabbed her, tried to hold her back; but Mrs Mullarkey was possessed and hardly seemed to notice. She raised the rolling pin out of Bansi's reach, flung her off and advanced relentlessly on her friend.

'Hey, missus!' A voice came from knee-height. Mrs Mullarkey glanced down. 'Can I interest you in a biscuit?' Pogo enquired savagely, swinging the poker at her shins.

Mrs Mullarkey collapsed like a puppet whose strings have been sliced through.

Pogo looked down at her. 'Ha!' he mocked. 'Just think what I could do if I existed!' He met Granny's worried gaze. 'You needn't look at me like that, missus. She'll wake up with a bruised shinbone, but she'll be fine otherwise.'

'Fine? When you've knocked her out?'

'By hitting her on the leg? Have some sense, missus! I just broke the spell, that's all.' Pogo sighed irritably, as if tired of having to explain things to ignorant mortals. 'It's like she was put into a kind of magical sleep, see; and then her body was taken over by the enchantment. Take away the enchantment – by belting her one with an iron poker, for instance – and all that's left is the sleep. She'll feel better after a wee doze.'

'Now, talking of that enchantment . . .' Granny began suspiciously.

'Don't go blaming that on me!' Pogo snapped. 'If it's anyone's fault, it's your own. Oh, don't pull that shocked face. *Nora Maura Margaret Mullarkey!*' he mimicked. 'That wolf is a warrior of the Dark Sidhe! And you spoke your friend's full name in front of him, giving him the power to enchant her! Have you no sense?'

'Aye, and have you none either, Pogo?' a voice enquired good-humouredly. 'Wasting time arguing with mortals when there's work to be done!'

There, perched cheerfully on the windowsill – though no one had seen him appear – was a boy of about Bansi's own age, dressed in colours which seemed to dance like firelight. His face was wildly handsome, with the merriest smile Bansi had ever seen; it was the sort of face, she felt, that you couldn't help liking.

Granny clearly didn't feel the same way. 'Here!' she said, snatching up the poker. 'And who might this be, Mr Brownie? Friend of yours?'

'I suppose, aye,' Pogo growled ungraciously. 'This is Tam. He's with me. He's the púca I told you about,' he added to Bansi, as the boy leaped lithely through the window and landed with a mirthful, mocking bow to all present.

'A púca?' Granny asked sharply. 'No offence meant, young man, but if you're a púca, shouldn't you be a bit more . . . well . . . goaty-looking?'

'Granny!' Bansi exclaimed, embarrassed by her granny's rudeness. But as Tam burst out laughing Bansi blushed deeper, for she realized she had no idea at all of what would seem rude to a faery.

'No, maybe I should, now,' Tam chuckled, heedless of Pogo's obvious disapproval and sense of urgency. 'Good idea, missus. All the goat stuff's great craic, so it is. How's this?'

Granny shrieked and snatched up the poker, waving it furiously at the muscular goat-headed man who had suddenly appeared in Tam's place. 'Bansi!' she ordered. 'Don't look!'

At the same time, Pogo was shouting, 'Tam, stop messing about, now! And for goodness' sakes, get some clothes on! Cover that thing up!'

The goat-headed man laughed again, a great

booming guffaw that almost shook the room. 'Not to your liking, missus?' he asked. 'How's this, then?' Next second, he was an enormous shaggy black goat, taller than Granny, with gleaming yellow eyes. '*Meeeh!*' he said. 'How's that? Is that better?'

Granny stepped back in alarm, standing over her unconscious friend protectively, but Bansi, feeling perfectly safe, stifled a laugh. It seemed obvious to her – though she didn't know how – that Tam was good-hearted, however wild and carefree a spirit he might be.

The goat laughed again, and next moment was once more a tousle-haired boy in flame-coloured clothing. 'No, to be honest, this is more me, missus. The goat stuff's good fun and all, mind, but when I'm not up to mischief this is how I prefer to look. Is that all right by you?' He winked at Bansi, who grinned back.

'Well, I never . . .' Granny began, looking shocked.

'Come on, Granny, you started it!' Bansi teased. Somehow Tam's very presence had lightened her mood, distracted her from the danger. 'You were the one who said he should be more goaty!'

'Well, that's what all the old stories say about the púca,' Granny grumbled. 'I may not be an expert like Nora, but I know enough to have heard how the púca takes the shape of a goat . . .'

'Never mind all that!' Pogo raged. 'Here you all are, feeding Tam's pride by talking about nothing but him, when there's a warrior of the Dark Sidhe on the loose and the child's very life is in danger!'

Granny went pale. 'What–?' she began.

'I'm not going through all that again,' the brownie said, glaring at her. 'The short version, missus, is that the Lord of the Dark Sidhe wants to sacrifice your wee girl in order to become more powerful, and we're here to stop him doing that. Except goaty-boy hasn't been much help so far.'

'Here!' Tam objected, still grinning all over his face. 'I resent that, wee man. I've been out there all night keeping the wolf from the door!'

'Well, you didn't manage to keep it from the window, did you?' Granny snapped.

Tam shrugged cheerfully. 'Is that why it's such a mess in here? I'd have thought you'd have sorted that out by now, Pogo. Still, no harm done, eh?'

Pogo looked like he might explode. 'No *harm* done? The Dark Sidhe broke in here, paralysed the girl and bewitched the old biddy on the floor there! *Twice* they've been in mortal danger, Tam; twice the Dark Sidhe have nearly had the Blood of the Morning Stars in their hands, and all you can say is "no harm done"! Where *were* you? It was your job to guard the house and stop that wolf-warrior from ever getting in!'

'Aye, well, he was a bit craftier than I thought, see. Suddenly looked up like he'd heard something, and raced off, so I followed him – I know, I know,' he added, as Pogo opened his mouth to speak, 'I should've just stayed at my post, but I was getting bored. So anyway, I kept on his tail, even when he took cover in some woodland – couldn't see him through the trees, but I could hear him moving all right. Except, when he finally broke cover, it wasn't him. It was a fox. He's clever, I'll give him that – he must have startled it, got it running, gone to ground till I was off on a wild goose chase and then doubled back. Could have kicked myself when I realized. Still, here I am, and delighted to make your acquaintance, by the way,' he added with a merry grin and another bow, this one all for Bansi, who found herself giggling most uncharacteristically. 'Tam's the name, and as long as I'm here, you've no need to fear!'

Bansi almost giggled again, but kept it inside. *Stop it!* she told herself. *Have a bit of dignity!* Ignoring the glare her granny was shooting at the faery boy, she put on her most grown-up manner and held her hand out. 'I'm Bansi,' she said. 'Pleased to meet you.'

Tam took her hand, but instead of shaking it he bowed again, a low, courtly bow like an Elizabethan gentleman, and kissed her hand gently and only half mockingly. Just in time, Bansi caught another giggle that threatened to bubble to the surface. *Honestly*, she thought, *you're behaving like Preeti!*

The thought that she could be anything like her silly, twittery, pink-obsessed cousin so irritated her that she snatched her hand away.

'Right – what do we do now?' she asked Tam.

He straightened up, with yet another grin and a wink. 'Ah, we just wait it out, I reckon.'

'Wait it out?' Pogo fumed. 'Why, you stupid—'

'Think about it, now, Pogo. There's only one of them.'

'As far as we know,' Pogo broke in sourly.

'As far as we know,' Tam agreed cheerfully. 'The way I see it, if we all just sit tight till nightfall, we're in the clear. To be honest, it's easier now these mortals know about us; we can stay here and guard Bansi without any of that hiding rigmarole. As long as we can do that, we've won. To fulfil the prophecy, they need the Blood of the Morning Stars, joined together and flowing, and where can they find that except in her veins? It's not like they can mix some up themselves, now, is it?'

For a moment, Bansi was only aware of a deep and sudden sense of unease. Something was badly wrong; there was something they'd overlooked, and it had to do with what Tam had just said. It took a second for it to burrow into Bansi's mind; but when it did, it exploded.

'Gran! Where are Mum and Dad?'

'Well, they're in bed, love . . .' A look of puzzlement came over the old woman's face. 'But they can't still be asleep, surely? There's been enough noise here tonight to wake the dead!'

Gripped by a sudden panic, Bansi raced across the landing and tore open the door to her parents' room. There, a dreadful sight met her eyes.

The room was in utter disarray, showing every sign of a violent struggle. The window was smashed; the bedding was lying crumpled and torn upon the floor.

Of her parents, there was no sign.

Chapter Nine

Bansi stood for a moment in shock, her mind racing. Everything that Pogo had told her about the prophecy tumbled in her head, echoing together with Tam's words.

When the Blood of the Morning Stars, joined and flowing together, is returned at last to the sacred earth . . .

'It's not like they can mix some up themselves, now, is it?'

It made sense.

'Pogo,' she said, 'they've got my parents!' Behind her, she heard her grandmother gasp.

'Don't be ridiculous, girl. What would they want with . . .' Pogo's voice tailed off as realization dawned. 'Ah, *no*!'

'What?' Tam asked, appearing behind them.

'If my mum's descended from Avalloc,' Bansi said, 'and my dad from Caer . . .'

'Ah, now, that's not playing fair!' said Tam. 'They're going to spill your *parents*' blood?'

'It's still the Blood of the Morning Stars,' Bansi

pointed out. 'And if–' She stopped, unable to face where the thought was leading.

Pogo faced it for her. 'If they sacrifice them together, they can make sure the blood's joined and flowing as one by the time it reaches the ground.'

Bansi swallowed, feeling suddenly sick. Little black dots swam in front of her eyes, and for one horrible second she thought she might faint. Pictures crowded into her mind: dreadful images of her parents bound or chained, with sharp blades or animal teeth pricking at their throats, and as fast as she pushed one picture aside another took its place.

'Ah, well, on the bright side,' Tam said, 'my guess is it'll do them no good. It's Bansi they need, right enough.'

'Bright side!' Granny gasped in outrage and horror. 'They're going to kill my son and his lovely wife, and you're looking on the bright side!' Her face took on a furious look. 'Oh, I have not *words* to describe these hallions! Kidnappers and murderers! Well, how do we stop them? What do we do?'

Pogo looked at Bansi. His little face creased and wrinkled, but for once he had nothing to say. Bansi stared back, looking for some kind of comfort or reassurance in the brownie's eyes, but found none.

'There's one thing that might work,' Tam offered. 'But it's up to you, Bansi. How brave are you feeling?'

Bansi was surprised to find that she was feeling very brave indeed. Brave, and frightened, and furious and determined. She looked Tam in the eye and felt strengthened by what she saw there. 'Tell me what to do,' she said.

'Well,' the púca said, 'the Dark Lord plans to fulfil the prophecy by sacrificing your parents – not that that'll work, mind; but still. Now, if *we* were to fulfil the prophecy first . . .'

'Tam, no!' Pogo interrupted, a look of fury on his little face.

'Pogo, just think before you start arguing!' Tam said. 'I know what you're going to say – no brownie would put a mortal in such danger. Right?' Pogo nodded sourly. 'But by doing nothing, you're condemning *two* mortals to death, aren't you? This way, we can make sure no harm comes to Bansi, and maybe save her parents, too. Besides which – are you completely sure that what he's planning has *no* chance of working? Imagine the consequences if it did!'

Pogo subsided. He folded his arms in grudging resignation and glared at the floor. 'Aye. Well,' he said after a moment, 'maybe you're right, Tam. I don't like it; but maybe you're right. Maybe it's the only way left to us now.'

'What *are* the pair of you blethering on about?' Granny burst out.

Pogo turned to her exasperatedly. 'The only way we might stop the Dark Lord sacrificing your son and his wife,' he said, 'is to act first, and fulfil the prophecy ourselves.'

'You're not suggesting sacrificing my wee Bansi!' Granny exclaimed, pointing angrily with the poker.

'No, missus, no,' Tam soothed. 'That's the irony of it – no sacrifice is needed. All Bansi has to do is come and stand in one of the sacred places of Tir na n'Óg. That's all. We can take her straight to our friends as soon as dawn begins to break; there's a sacred grove less than a mile from where we'll be meeting them. The prophecy can be fulfilled in minutes and the child returned home by nightfall.'

'Oh, aye?' Granny raised a cynical eyebrow. 'And this Dark Lord fellow'll just let Fintan and Asha go, then?'

Tam shrugged wryly. 'Well, you never know. Thing is, no one's sure what'll happen when the prophecy's fulfilled. But I reckon the one who claims the inheritance of Derga–'

'And that'll be you, will it?' Granny asked sceptically.

Tam grinned, impervious to the insult. 'Most likely it'll be Caithne of the Sacred Grove; and maybe she'll come into such power straight away that she'll be able to stop the sacrifice from happening. Or maybe not, but whatever happens, it should give us an advantage.

'And you never know – maybe if we get there first, the Dark Lord'll know somehow – could be the whole of Tir na n'Óg'll know as soon as it happens. And maybe once they're of no use to him he *will* let them go.'

Granny glared. 'Or maybe he'll . . .' She stopped, unable to bring herself to finish the sentence. The unspoken words, *kill them anyway*, hung in the air.

Tam shrugged again. 'Maybe he will. I'm not saying for certain we'll get them back for you, missus. But if we try, then we might. And if we don't try, then we won't.'

Bansi took a deep breath. She felt shaky inside; but the faces of her parents filled her mind and spurred her on. 'Let's go, then,' she said.

'Bansi! No! I forbid it!' Granny ordered, shocked. 'How could I look your father in the eye and tell him I'd let you go off to the land of the Good People?'

'Granny, I don't think I've got any choice. If I don't go, you'll never get the chance to look him in the eye. We'll never see Dad or Mum again.' She turned to Tam. 'Do you need to do any magic to open the gate?'

'Not from this side,' Tam answered. 'We just have to enter the stone circle during the twilight of dawn. But if you're willing to do this, then we'd better get going. Listen.'

In the distance, a cock was crowing.

Bansi had long since made her decision. 'Give me a minute,' she said. 'Wait for me downstairs.'

Granny followed her into her room. 'Bansi, it's madness,' she said, stepping carefully round Mrs Mullarkey, who was still lying peacefully where she had fallen. 'You can't go!'

Bansi pulled her jeans on and reached for a turquoise fleece. 'I've got to, Granny,' she said. 'It's our only chance of getting Mum and Dad back.'

'Please, sweetheart. I . . . couldn't stand if it I lost you as well as your father.'

Bansi's eyes grew warm as the tears began to well up. 'Gran . . . I have to. I'm sorry.' She stepped forward and put her arms around her grandmother.

Granny enfolded her in a warm embrace. 'I love you, darling. And I'm sorry as well.' Tears welled in her own old eyes as she let go and turned to leave.

'You don't have anything to be sorry about, Granny. I love you, too.'

The old woman smiled ruefully at her as she closed the door.

As Bansi was putting her trainers on, she heard the key turn in the lock.

'Granny! No!' Suddenly frantic, Bansi reached the door too late. 'Granny!' She twisted the handle, pulled with all her might, but in vain. 'Let me out!'

On the other side of the door, a tear ran down each of Eileen O'Hara's wrinkled cheeks; but the old woman's face was resolute. 'I'm sorry, love. I'm so sorry. But I can't let you. I can't.' She slipped the key into her cardigan pocket and started down the stairs, wiping her eyes.

In stubborn desperation, Bansi looked around the room. Her eyes fixed on the shattered window frame; and beyond it, the branches of a tree.

Downstairs, Granny O'Hara squared up to Pogo.

'Go! Get out! You're not taking my granddaughter anywhere! I wish I'd never set eyes on any of you! You go back to wherever you came from, and you just rescue my son and his wife!'

Pogo scowled. 'Without your granddaughter, we've no chance of that.'

'Aye, and if you take her, I'll have no family left at all, will I? Get out!' Furious, beyond reason, she aimed a kick at the little man, who skipped nimbly out of the way.

* * *

Upstairs, Bansi was carefully opening what was left of the window, taking care to avoid the jagged shards of glass that protruded from the broken frame. That done, she bent to pick up the poker and thrust it like a sword through her belt. Climbing onto the sill and balancing like a gymnast, she poised to jump. She stared at the tree branch, mentally measuring the distance she needed to clear.

She leaped.

Below, Tam looked up and grinned.

'You realize you're condemning your son to death?' Pogo asked harshly.

'Don't you dare put that on me, little man! Don't you *dare*! I will *not* be made responsible for what you people have done to my family! And I will *not* lose my granddaughter as well as my son!'

'Ready?' Tam whispered, as Bansi clambered down through the branches and dropped lightly to the ground. She nodded, not trusting herself to speak; a lump was rising in her throat. 'Just turn your back, then.' He noticed the poker hanging at her hip. 'And keep that thing away from me.'

Bansi turned. There was a movement behind her; she felt herself abruptly lifted away from the ground.

Suddenly, without quite knowing how, she was astride the back of a huge night-black horse. It tossed back its great head, rearing and stamping frighteningly.

Granny and Pogo were glaring furiously at each other, both breathing hard and too angry for words, when from outside there came a wild neighing. Both heads turned.

'Right, well, I'll be off then,' Pogo said hurriedly. 'Um, thanks for having us, missus – I'll see myself out.' He bolted for the door.

'What on earth . . . ? Now just wait a moment!' Granny barked, giving chase. 'Where do you think you're—? Oh, my . . .'

Her voice faded weakly. There, standing right in front of her house, was the biggest horse she'd ever seen; an enormous black stallion with burning yellow eyes. Pogo was scurrying nimbly up its flank; and already sitting astride it and holding on for grim death was her son's daughter.

'Bansi!' she yelled. 'Get off that thing at once!' She snatched up the iron skillet, which had fallen on the gravel beneath Bansi's window, and glared furiously at the horse; the great black beast reared and whinnied like a thing possessed. 'Put her down!' she screeched. 'Give me my granddaughter!'

The horse reared once more. Sparks flashed as its hooves struck the ground. Suddenly, nightmarishly, it was bearing down on her.

Chapter Ten

'No!' screamed Bansi. Before her, Granny gripped the skillet with both hands and raised it to shoulder-height, ready to strike the horse even as it ran her down.

At the last moment it leaped, high into the air. Bansi felt her stomach lurch; she looked down to see her grandmother standing dazed, skillet lifted uselessly, far below. For an instant, time seemed to pause . . .

With a heavy jolt, they landed. Gravel spun beneath gleaming hooves. Down the driveway and across the road they hurtled, hurdling the hedge on the other side. Across fields and hills they raced, faster and faster, with Tam never seeming to draw breath or grow tired. The moonlight shone down coldly from high above them, but already the stars were fading against the coming morning. On the horizon a thin, bright line shone through the dark blue.

* * *

Granny didn't pause for more than a moment. Taking the key from her pocket, she raced up the stairs and unlocked Bansi's room. Nora Mullarkey was still lying there, sleeping peacefully on the floor where she had fallen.

'Iron,' Eileen O'Hara muttered. 'That's what'll do it. I hope.' Feverishly, she knelt and placed the skillet on her friend's chest. Taking hold of her hands, she pressed them against the cold metal.

'Wake up,' she muttered. 'Come on, Nora! Wake up!'

There was no response.

'Nora, *please*!' She lifted the pan and touched it gently to the sleeping face. Nora Mullarkey let out a loud snore.

'Nora! Come on, you silly old fool!'

Again she placed the pan on Mrs Mullarkey's chest and laid the wrinkled hands on it.

Nothing.

Eileen O'Hara looked out of the window. From where she knelt, she could see the hint of an unwelcome glow beginning to creep over the eastern hills. She moaned softly, thinking of her son now lost to her, and her granddaughter as good as.

'I'll thank you not to call me a silly old fool, Eileen O'Hara! And to keep your old kitchenware off my best cardigan, come to that!'

Granny turned. Nora Mullarkey was sitting up, a harsh, if slightly woozy expression on her face, the skillet held loosely in one hand as the other absently rubbed her shin.

'Nora! Thank goodness! There's still time!'

'Time for what, you daft old haddock?'

'The . . . the Good People – they took Fintan and Asha, and then Bansi went after them on a big magic horse . . .'

'A big magic horse–?' With a gasp, Mrs Mullarkey clasped one wrinkled hand to her mouth. 'You don't mean to tell me she's ridden off on one of *their* steeds?'

'Aye – well, I think it was the boy, the púca – he turns into things . . .'

'A *púca*? Oh, my goodness, Eileen!' Her eyes began to well with tears of sympathy for her friend. 'I am *so, so* sorry! Bansi was such a lovely wee girl . . .'

Granny stood suddenly, eyes blazing, and glared down at her friend. 'What do you mean, "*was*"? She *is* a lovely wee girl, Nora Mullarkey!'

Mrs Mullarkey flushed with embarrassment. 'Well, yes, of course, Eileen . . . what I mean is, you'll miss her so much . . .'

If Granny' eyes had blazed before, they were now on the point of explosion. She leaned forward angrily, her face reddening fiercely. '*Miss* her, Nora? *MISS* her? We're not going to *miss* her; we're going to *find* her!'

Mrs Mullarkey's mouth fell open in astonishment. 'Talk some sense, Eileen! You know where they'll have taken them – to . . . to the place they come from! It wouldn't be safe to try and follow them, now would it . . . ?'

Granny furiously stamped her foot on the floor.

'*Not safe?* This is my *family*, Nora! My wee boy! His wee girl and her mother!' The foot stamped again, and again with every exclamation. '*They're* not safe! And if you think I'm going to sit here and wait while they're in mortal peril off in Faeryland, then—'

'Have you no sense, Eileen O'Hara?!?' Mrs Mullarkey cried, leaping to her feet. 'Using *that* word, after all you've seen? Do you want that wolf-creature and all its friends howling at the door?'

'*I DON'T CARE!!!* They can *all* come, every blessed faery in the world – no, I will *not* stop saying it, Nora, *faery faery faery!* – and when they all come then I'll beat them black and blue with an iron horse-shoe until they tell me where my wee Bansi is!'

'*Stop* it, Eileen! Foolishness won't bring them back!'

'No, Nora, and nor will cowardice, neither! All these years you've always made yourself out so brave and fierce, striking fear into the heart of every shopkeeper in Ballyfey, and here you are, too scared of the faeries to help when my family's in mortal danger!'

'I am *not* scared!'

'You are too, Nora Mullarkey! You're a big frightened chicken, that's all *you* are! You're too scared of the faeries to even say the word!'

The challenge hung in the air between them like a slap in the face. In the sudden silence, it echoed like a cymbal.

Mrs Mullarkey drew in a slow breath. For a moment her face was a rigid mask of anger. Then, 'Faery!' she yelled. 'All right, Eileen O'Hara? FAERY! FAERY, FAERY, *FAERY!* I can say it louder than you, because I'm *not* scared!'

'You can *not* say it louder, Nora Mullarkey, because for all your pretending to be brave, you're still frightened the *faeries* will come and get you!'

'If the *faeries* come here they'll get a taste of this frying pan where it hurts most!'

'Load of *rubbish*, Nora Mullarkey! First sign of a *faery* and you'd be out that door, dropping my frying pan behind you! You're a coward! Otherwise you'd come with me to help me rescue my wee Bansi!'

Mrs Mullarkey looked scandalized. 'Eileen O'Hara! You must be losing your mind, or your hearing, or something of the kind! Not go? Why, if I don't go to save little Bansi, then who will? I couldn't expect a frail wee old lady like yourself to, that's for certain.'

Granny O'Hara nearly hit the roof.

'*Frail?* Nora, that's rich, coming from someone who's seen much better days! In fact, you must forgive me, I was forgetting how fragile you are these days, I couldn't possibly ask you to go–'

'*Fragile???* That's it, Eileen O'Hara, out of my way! I'm getting in that car and I'm off to . . . to *Faery*land this very minute!' Mrs Mullarkey turned and dashed down the stairs. Granny quickly followed, trying to overtake just as they reached the front door, with the result that they spent several seconds jammed side by side in the doorway, struggling like cats in a sack before popping like corks into the dimness of the garden. Glaring at one another, they hurried to the green Morris Minor, wrenched open the doors and flung themselves in.

Moments later they leaped from the car again and ran for the nearby garage. With more speed than you would have thought possible, they produced several battered old boxes and loaded them into the boot.

It was only a few minutes afterwards that Sean McKnight, startled from sleep, instinctively threw himself sideways at the roar of a familiar engine on the road outside, and fell out of bed. As he clutched his forehead in agony, he could just make out the sound of two elderly ladies yelling their heads off at each other. It sounded, though he couldn't be sure, as if they were shouting about fairies.

'They're *away* with the fairies, the pair of them,' he groaned.

Like a great shadowy ghost Slieve Donnan loomed over Bansi in the grey half-darkness.

'There!' Pogo pointed to an indistinct shape on the hillside, growing closer by the second. 'That's the stone circle, around the ancient oak. Now make sure you hang on tight. We have to enter the circle together if we want to arrive together.'

Bansi chewed her lip and made no reply. She wound her fingers into Tam's mane and concentrated on the relentless pounding of his hooves against the soil.

'The devil!' Nora Mullarkey exclaimed, as Eileen O'Hara – a little calmer now – reached the end of her explanation. 'So he used my own name against me! Well, he'll not do that again! Hang on, Eileen, I've just got to make a wee detour!'

The dark green Morris Minor Traveller swerved suddenly and made off down a narrow lane, its driver heedless of her passenger's protests.

They were higher now, and Bansi could make out the shape of the stones around the ancient tree a little below the hilltop. To her eyes, they were shimmering and glowing – much as the whole hill had appeared to do on the previous evening. She shuddered, half tempted to leap from the horse's back; but then a picture of her parents came into her mind, and she clenched her jaw and sat firm.

They had almost reached the stones – the ground was levelling out under the pounding hooves – when a movement in the great oak tree caught her eye. It was a bird on a low branch – a raven. Black ragged wings flapping like a danger flag, it cawed harshly in wild alarm. Bansi's stomach chilled; turning, she caught a glimpse of movement. Something large and grey broke from cover, moving at speed, closing on them from behind. She tried to shout a warning.

Too late. As Tam leaped, so too did the wolf. Propelling itself in a great arc that intersected theirs, it tore Bansi from the horse's back. She had one confused glimpse of Pogo staring in horror at her; saw the gleaming hooves strike the earth within the faery ring. The great stallion, bearing its tiny rider, disappeared.

A second later she, too, struck the earth, hard, and everything went black.

Chapter Eleven

Eileen O'Hara heaved an impatient and anxious sigh as the door of the big old house at last opened and Nora Mullarkey hurried out.

'If we don't get there before dawn I swear I will *never* forgive you!' she grumbled anxiously, as her friend settled back into the driver's seat and gunned the engine. 'Making social calls when my wee girl's in danger!'

'We'll get there, all right,' Mrs Mullarkey assured her tersely as the little car jerked and shot forward. 'I was only a couple of minutes. And that was no social call, I can tell you. I'm ready to face that wolf-boy now, and he won't get the better of me this time.'

Eileen O'Hara rolled her eyes despairingly. 'What could a few minutes with the parish priest have possibly done to make any difference at all?'

Nora Mullarkey glanced disdainfully at her friend, oblivious to how wildly the car swerved. 'Eileen, you're the big-mouth that blabbed my name in front of one of the Good People. Do you think I'm going to go spilling my secrets to you now?'

She jerked the steering wheel savagely. The car skidded sharply as it swerved round the corner to rejoin the main road.

Time flows differently in the Other Realm; so it may have been just then, or it may not, that a dark shadow in the gloom of a great and ancient stone ruin suddenly opened like a flower. In an instant it had bloomed and blossomed into the shape of a tiny brown man riding a huge black stallion, which emerged at a canter and swiftly brought itself up short. Even as it stopped, the horse was already changing back into a tousle-haired, handsome, wild-looking boy. Pogo slid down from Tam's shoulder and stood by his side.

One by one, other figures began to emerge from the gloom, until the two were surrounded by a motley collection of faery beings. Some looked almost human, but others were odd and otherworldly in appearance. There were little people – some of them brown, although not brownies, others green, grey, or even purple; some reached to Tam's waist, while others were no bigger than his finger. There were hunched and twisted goblins; tall, stately dryads; squat, dwarfish creatures with burning red eyes; slender, willowy elves with delicate blue complexions.

Silently they pressed in around Pogo and Tam.

'You failed, then,' said one, a goblin with wrinkled skin the colour of mottled stone.

'Ah, well, now, I wouldn't exactly say "failed",' Tam began cheerily.

'What *would* you say?' the goblin retorted. 'You were supposed to guard the child – to stay near her and protect her. So where is she? Maybe she's fulfilled the prophecy already, and we're all safe? Hah!' He spat derisively on the broken stone floor at Tam's feet. 'Or maybe you just changed your minds? The mortal realm too much for you, was it?'

'There was a change of plan,' Pogo answered, his tone equally harsh. 'The Dark Sidhe have the girl's parents.'

There was a shocked pause as the news sank in.

'No!' whispered a delicate sylph, her voice sighing like a sorrowful breeze. 'Could the prophecy be fulfilled in such a way? Then all is lost!'

'So why did you not bring the girl?' asked a small grey imp with sunken eyes. 'Let me guess. She refused to come, even with her parents in peril of their lives. What did I tell you? Mortals! Good for nothing!' There were nods and a murmuring of agreement from some of the others.

'No!' Pogo spoke sharply. 'Mortals are like us. Some are good, some are bad, and some' – here he glared at the imp who had spoken – 'are stupid. This girl is good, and brave, and of royal blood, too – the Blood of the Morning Stars.'

'Where is she, then?' a beautiful, blue-skinned elf-woman challenged. 'If she's so noble, why has she not come to fulfil the prophecy and so try to save her parents?'

Pogo glowered up at her. 'She was with us,' he said, 'and willing to help. But a warrior of the Dark Sidhe separated us as we reached the gate, and we lost her.' He stared defiantly around the circle as a despairing groan went up.

'I told you!' snarled one, who looked like a tall, red-headed man. 'I *said* we couldn't rely on a púca! We should never have let that brownie think that . . .'

He fell silent as an elegant dryad stepped forward. Her skin was a deep brown, textured like bark, and her hair fell in green fronds around her face.

'We all agreed,' she said firmly, her voice like the rustling of leaves. 'We agreed to send two to protect the child until she was of age, and then to bring her to Tir na n'Óg only if she was willing. You also agreed, Aed Firetongue,' she added, as the red-headed man opened his mouth to speak again. 'And we sent Pogo and Tam as the two best suited to the task. Can you assure me beyond doubt that you would have succeeded where they failed?'

The red-headed man hesitated. 'No, Caithne of the Sacred Grove, but—'

Caithne interrupted him. Although her voice was not loud, it commanded utter respect. 'Then to argue is vain as well as useless. Our task now is clear: we must try to find this girl before it's too late – if it is not too late already.'

'It won't be,' Tam assured them. Alone of the whole company, he showed no signs of solemnity. 'We touched the earth within the circle before she did, didn't we, Pogo?'

The brownie nodded. 'Only by moments, but we did. I'm sure of it.'

'So she won't be through the gate yet – and maybe not for hours, if fortune's with us. When she does arrive in Tir na n'Óg, we've as good a chance of finding her as the Dark Lord does.' The púca looked round at the company, clearly enjoying the attention and not in the least put out by the many hostile stares. 'It's still early, isn't it?'

Caithne nodded. 'The sun is barely risen.'

Tam grinned. 'Couldn't be better. The Blood of the Morning Stars must be returned to the sacred earth as the light dies. They won't attempt any sacrifice till dusk. We've got the whole day to find them.'

'Aye, and to rescue the child *and* her parents from

the hordes of the Dark Sidhe. How likely is that?' the small grey imp objected.

Pogo rounded on him. 'Likely or not, Bindweed, we're going to do it. Or die trying. If the Dark Sidhe fulfil the prophecy and obtain the blessing, we're all slaves or dead anyway. And it won't ever be said of me that I left a mortal child to bleed to death at the knife of my enemy without I did all I could to save her. Now if you want to crawl off home, do it! Off you go! But if you're with us, then shut your mouth and do something useful for once!'

The imp fell silent and looked away sullenly.

'Anyway,' Tam added, 'we don't have to rescue them all. If we can find the girl and get her to one of the sacred places before sundown, it'll make no difference if they sacrifice her parents after that. Or, if we find the parents and we can fulfil the prophecy with them after all, then no matter if they kill the girl.'

Pogo cast him a look full of contempt and disgust. 'No matter? *No matter?*' he spat furiously.

The dryad spoke again; quietly, but with such presence that the whole room stilled. 'Pogo, Tam is right. We are nothing but a collection of solitary faeries and little people, less powerful than the smallest tribe in the whole of Tir na n'Óg. If the Dark Sidhe have been so careless that even we know about their plans for the child of the Blood of the Morning

Stars, who else knows? Who else is even now looking for the girl? The Gwyllion? The Unseelie Court? At the moment, this land exists in an uneasy peace – but should any of these increase their power, the balance will tip in their favour. We will be plunged into war, which can only end with a tyrant standing triumphant over the realm of Faery. One mortal life is nothing against such a future.'

'All this I know, Caithne of the Sacred Grove,' Pogo said quietly.

'Yes, Pogo, you do,' Caithne replied. 'Of course you feel for the mortals – you would be no true brownie otherwise. I called you here, however, not to save the girl's life, but to save our land. And once the prophecy is fulfilled, the land is either safe or doomed – regardless of the mortals' fate.' Her voice rose, including all of them. 'Go, now. The destiny of Tir na n'Óg is in your hands. Find the girl or her parents. Lead them to one of the sacred places. Good fortune be with us all.'

She raised her branch-like arms in blessing, and the faery creatures bowed respectfully. Then, in twos and threes, they vanished into the shadows and slipped away.

'We'd best be off, Pogo,' Tam said, turning to his partner. But the brownie had vanished, too.

Tam sighed, and made his way outside into the

early morning light. Pogo was standing on a tumbled wall among the boulders and stones of the ruined buildings, gazing angrily across the landscape.

'We won't find her by standing about here all day,' Tam observed cheerily.

Pogo spun round fiercely, to glare at Tam. 'If you think I'm coming with you, after what you just said . . .'

'Ah, come on, Pogo.' Tam grinned as broadly as ever, unfazed by the brownie's anger. 'No one's got a better chance of finding Bansi than we do, if we work together.'

'And what do you care about finding her?' Pogo growled. ' "No matter if they kill the girl", he says! Typical púca! Selfish to the core!'

'For goodness sake, wee man! I was just trying to encourage the others, that's all! Me, though? Of course I care about finding her. For one thing, there's the prophecy to think about. But besides that, she's a brave girl and I'm not going to let her down. Nor her parents, either, before you ask.'

Pogo made no answer. He glowered furiously.

'Come on, Pogo,' Tam tried again. 'You've got the instinct; I've got the magic. There's no better team!'

'I don't care,' Pogo hissed. 'I'd sooner work with anyone else!'

'Anyone?' asked a cheery little voice. 'Grand! Let'sh get going, Pogo me boy!'

Tam grinned.

Pogo closed his eyes despairingly. 'Oh, no,' he said, 'Flooter, don't tell me that's you . . .'

'All right, it'sh me Uncle Bob!' the voice declared proudly. 'And a very fine uncle he is, too.' A little red cap peeped up over the stony edge of a low fragment of wall, and then suddenly disappeared again. 'Whoopsh!' the voice muttered. 'It's more shlippery than I th . . . thought. Try again, Flooter . . . here we go . . .'

The cap reappeared, followed by a merry little grey face with a very red nose and cheeks. 'Nearly there . . . hang on, now . . .' the little man continued, hauling himself up to the top of the ruined wall. 'There we go!' he said, as he reached the summit. 'Whoopsh!' he repeated cheerfully as he fell off backwards. There was a dull thump from the soil below. 'Ah – hang on, now,' Flooter continued, undaunted. 'I know – I'll go round the front.'

'Take that grin off your face, Tam,' Pogo snapped, leaping from his perch as Flooter wavered into view and tottered towards them.

'Ah, sorry, Pogo,' Tam said. 'I'll just leave you and Flooter to it, shall I?'

'No!'

Tam was enjoying this. 'But you said—'

'I don't care what I said! I am *not* working with a

cluricaun! Look at him! It's barely sunrise and he's drunk already!'

Flooter, offended, drew himself up to his full height. Since he only reached to Pogo's chin, this wasn't very impressive. 'Any drink shtill in me is left over from the night before!' he said, waving a little bottle in Pogo's face, and at much of the air on either side of it, too. 'I haven't touched a drop in hoursh!' He took an absent-minded swig, and then stared at the bottle, bemused. 'Now where did *that* come from?' he asked himself. He tasted it again, and his eyes lit up.

'Well, Pogo,' Tam pointed out, 'it's him or me. Take your choice!'

Pogo turned on him. 'Not a word more from you. Not a word! And I swear, when we find Bansi you'd better protect her with your life.'

Flooter raised his bottle cheerily. 'Bansi, is that her name, then?' he slurred. 'Shame you losht her in the first place, Pogo. Shtill, I bet you left her house nice and clean, eh?'

Pogo, climbing onto Tam's shoulder, blushed a furious russet and did not look back. 'At least I didn't spend the night in her wine cellar, like some others might have done,' he muttered, as Tam feathered and took to the skies.

Flooter wobbled to his feet and stared after them. 'She has a wine cellar?' he asked.

* * *

Miles away and some time later, in a coldly magnificent galleried hall, a tall, sprawling figure lounged with elegant laziness across a grand and ornately carved double chair. Dimly flickering torches lit his cadaverously handsome face and cast strange black dancing shapes on the panelled walls around him. He yawned, stretched languorously and picked his teeth with a viciously bladed bone-white knife.

This done, he unpeeled himself from the chair with catlike fluidity. Suddenly, purposefully, he was striding the length of the great hall, his dark cloak billowing around him dramatically as his footsteps snapped hard on the floor tiles.

Before he reached the door a shadow appeared behind him, blooming and blossoming into the shape of a great grey wolf running at full speed as if landing after a mighty leap. The man stepped neatly and without apparent concern to one side; the wolf skidded, missing him by inches, its claws scrabbling for a hold on the smooth tiles.

Instantly the warriors who stood guard at the entrances to the room sprang forward, ready to attack; but the figure stopped them with a regal wave of his hand.

The wolf whimpered and abased itself before its master, who tutted impatiently.

'Oh, do stop whining, Conn. I'm not going to kill you for appearing in the wrong place.' As the wolf gratefully nuzzled his black-gloved hand, he suddenly seized its muzzle and forced it painfully upwards, adding, 'I might kill you for neglecting to bring the girl, though.' The point of the bone-white knife stroked the wolf's neck menacingly. 'So why don't you take that hearthrug off and tell me where she is?' With a twist of the wrist, he released the creature and affected an air of chilling patience.

The wolf carefully shrugged its pelt off, like a snake sloughing its skin, and Conn stood, head bowed.

'I tracked the púca and the brownie, Lord,' he said

quietly, 'and as you predicted, they led me to the girl.'

'Quite,' the Dark Lord agreed, examining his fingernails. With the knife point, he carefully flicked a speck of dirt out from underneath one of them. 'Obviously you had no way of finding the mortal child yourself, and since I have no pet brownie of my own, I arranged the next best thing.' He allowed himself a small, cold smile. 'Deceiving that arrogant tree-woman was not the easiest task I have ever set myself, Conn. I trust all my hard work hasn't been wasted. It would make me very . . . bad-tempered.'

The wolf-boy, fixed in his lord's bright, predatorial gaze, shuddered involuntarily. 'I followed the child to a mortal dwelling. The púca kept watch outside—'

'Now, Conn,' the Dark Lord interrupted silkily, 'I hope you're not going to tell me you were afraid to fight the púca?'

'No, Lord!' Conn protested. 'I was preparing to take him by surprise when for some reason the child's grandmother welcomed all of Faery to her home. Straightaway he left his post and entered the house himself, through an unlit window. I took my chance and struck. I seized the girl, but was overpowered by the use of iron. Still, I overheard the name of the old woman who bested me, and was able to bewitch her; but when I returned to claim the child, the púca became a horse and carried her off. I followed once more and snatched her from his back as he entered the stone circle, but she slipped from my grasp.'

The Lord of the Dark Sidhe grasped Conn's face, hard, with one hand, and again forced his gaze upwards.

'Really?' he asked. His voice carried a sharp, sceptical edge.

Unable to move his face, Conn glanced down with his eyes. 'Yes, Lord,' he said. 'I tore her garment with my teeth as I brought her down.'

'Indeed?' The tall man released his grip and looked down at the wolfskin. There was a scrap of turquoise fabric hanging from its lifeless mouth. Conn knelt and picked it up, offering it to his master.

'Mortal-made,' the Lord mused, rubbing the fleece material between his fingers. 'Clearly mortal-made. It will make her easier to hunt.' He paused for a moment, as if coming to a decision. 'You're sure she was separated from our enemies before entering the gate?'

Conn nodded.

'Very well, my young wolf; you have one last chance to redeem yourself. Take a guard of four warriors with you. Hunt the girl down and bring her to me, at Balor's Hollow, by sunset. Go!'

The boy bowed to his master. Then, quickly sweeping the wolfskin cloak over his shoulders, he fastened it at the throat and drew it around him as before. Within moments, he was the grey wolf once more. He pressed his nose to the scrap of fleece and sniffed, the smell of the garment and of its wearer filling his nostrils. He inhaled again, taking in the very essence of the material.

Then, with an animal grace, he turned swiftly and raced from the hall. As he did so, a figure slunk from the shadows and sidled up to the Lord of the Dark Sidhe.

'My Lord,' she said smoothly, 'once again, I must counsel against leaving such an important task in the hands – or, indeed the paws – of one so young.'

'And I suppose,' the Lord of the Dark Sidhe murmured, 'you think I would be so foolish as to entrust the task to you instead, and give you the opportunity to perform the sacrifice in my place? Conn may be young; he may be foolish; but he will bring the mortal child to me. The inheritance of Derga will be mine. No one else's. Once I have it, nobody – not even the Master of the Unseelie Court – will be able to stand against me. I, and I alone, will reign over Tir na n'Óg. You would do well to remember that, if you wish to see another sunrise.'

He turned, fixing her with coldly penetrating

yellow eyes, and smiled without mirth. The woman suppressed a shiver as she bowed and withdrew.

It may have been just then, or it may not, that the dark green Morris Minor Traveller was tearing up the narrow road towards the summit of Slieve Donnan, Mrs Mullarkey riding the accelerator hard with every twist and turn.

'Here we are!' she crowed as they screeched up towards the entrance to the car park, the rising sun at their backs. 'The viewpoint! We'll make it, I tell you!'

'No, Nora, we're too late! The sun's coming up! See?'

'The circle's on the other side of the hilltop,' Nora Mullarkey insisted. 'That side'll still be in the twilight shadows.'

'Not by the time we've parked the car, you silly old trout!'

Nora Mullarkey pressed her foot to the floor. 'Who said anything about parking?' she yelled, as the car accelerated into the car park and across the tarmac towards the railings on the far side. There was a loud crack; wood splintered all around them. Then the car was bumping and crashing down the grassy slope, juddering and jolting like some lunatic fairground ride from hell, bouncing and barrelling towards the stone circle.

'Nora! You'll kill us both!'

'Hold tight, Eileen! Here's where it gets bumpy!'

'Where it *gets—? Look out for those big rocks!'*

Nora Mullarkey steered towards a gap between two stones. Her foot rode the brake pedal. The car skidded. Suddenly, dangerously, it was out of control. Mrs Mullarkey wrestled wildly with the steering wheel.

'Nora! I don't think this counts as twilight any more!'

They slewed sideways; the car's rear wheel hit something; the vehicle spun madly into the air. The oak tree reeled across Eileen O'Hara's vision. Something black beat wild ragged wings against glass; she heard a harsh cawing; a window shattered. A thick overhanging branch forced its way in behind them, showering the women with splinters of glass and timber. Sky and earth and tree rolled insanely around them, whirling them towards oblivion. Eileen O'Hara screamed.

There was a sickening, crumpling crunch as they slammed into solid oak and struck the earth.

Chapter Twelve

Warmth. The sound of birdsong. The ferny smell of the forest floor.

Bansi slowly drifted up from the depths of unconsciousness, the blackness yielding to the soft orange of sunlight through closed eyelids. There was something hard and uncomfortable under her back, she realized.

And something alive wriggling inside her fleece.

She opened her eyes in sudden panic and looked around, forcing herself to keep as still as she could, taking stock of her situation. She was in a wide forest clearing . . . which meant that she wasn't in the stone circle . . . which meant that she must be in the Other Realm. The sun was high in the sky; either she'd been unconscious for hours, or time was different here. She was alone: no wolf ready to tear her throat out, but no Pogo or Tam to help her either. And there was some kind of animal – possibly dangerous, perhaps even deadly – squirming in her clothing. She held her breath and bit her lip, fighting off the temptation to jump up, scream, strike it with her hands. In her head, she pictured a scorpion ready to sting; but perhaps the animals here were much more vicious, much more lethal than anything she'd ever heard of. Her eyes flicked left, right, looking for something – anything – to use as a weapon. There was nothing. Then she remembered the poker. Her hand crept cautiously to her belt; grasped the ornate handle; pulled gently. It refused to move. The belt was twisted somehow, or perhaps the tip of the poker was stuck in the ground. In any case, she couldn't free it without a sharp movement. And that risked the creature – whatever it was – taking fright and striking.

Gingerly, Bansi raised her head just enough to see her stomach. A large, soft bulge marked the animal's movements under her fleece, torn where the wolf's teeth had ripped it. She watched the bump under the fabric move closer to the hole, and held her breath in the desperate hope that whatever it was would emerge, and fly or crawl or scuttle away.

And then something – its head, she guessed – began to show through the hole. It was red; or at least the tip was, although, as it continued to squeeze through, the red colour gave way to a grey, hairier surface – almost as if the thing was wearing a hat of some kind, Bansi thought. Then came arms: green, with grey paws – no, grey *hands*, she realized, and with that realization came the idea that this was some kind of little man. She let her breath out in a sigh of relief.

The little man turned, showing a bearded grey face with cherry-red nose and cheeks. He froze, his little bloodshot eyes widening with surprise.

'Oh – ah – um – oh, heavensh be praised, you're alive!' he blurted guiltily. 'I was just, um . . . I was just looking for a pulse, that's it, yes . . .'

'I don't normally keep my pulse in my belly,' Bansi observed dryly.

'Ah, well, that'd be it, glad to help, I'll be off then,' he gabbled, trying to squeeze his own little round belly through the hole without success. 'Umm . . . you couldn't give me a hand out of here now, young Bansi, could you?'

Bansi started. 'How do you know my name?'

'Do I? Oh, yesh, so I do. Very important things, names. Pleashed to meet you, by the way. You can call me Flooter. I'm a cluricaun,' he added proudly

'Um . . . yes, pleased to meet you, too, Flooter. But how *do* you know my name?'

'Oh, that. Pogo told me.'

Bansi sat up, causing Flooter to sway dangerously and pop out of the hole, landing in a heap on the forest floor. 'Pogo? Do you know where he is?'

The cluricaun sat up unsteadily. 'Let'sh see, now . . . an hour or so ago, he was way over that way shomewhere, in some old ruins.'

'Can you take me there?'

'No point, so there ishn't. He's not there any more. Gone off looking for you on the back of a swan. Courshe, it'sh not really a swan, it'sh a púca . . . Never trust a púca . . . Anyway, what was I saying? Oh, yes, even if he was shtill there it'd take you all day to get to him.'

'Then how did you get here so quickly?'

Flooter got to his feet. Swaying erratically, he looked up at Bansi and leaned closer. 'Nobody knows how the cluricaun travel,' he said, tapping his nose conspiratorially. He leaned in closer still, and lowered his voice. 'Not even,' he added, 'the cluricaun.' He tapped his nose again. On the third tap, he missed, lost his balance and fell over.

Bansi sighed. She was beginning to find Flooter a little exasperating.

'How did you find me, then?' she asked.

'Ah, well,' the cluricaun replied, sitting up again and taking out his little bottle, 'that'sh easy. I just thought that if you were in trouble, someone ought to look after the key to your wine cellar. Er . . . er . . . I mean, not that I was looking for it or anything, you undershtand, but . . .'

Bansi looked at the suddenly blushing Flooter. Understanding was beginning to come together in her mind; and with it, an idea.

'My . . . wine cellar,' she said slowly. 'So what you're saying is: even though you didn't know where I was, or what I looked like, or, well, *anything*, really, you were able to find me because you thought I had the key to a wine cellar?'

'That'sh it, Bansi, that'sh how it ish, and a very fine cellar I'm sure it . . . um, you do *have* the key, don't you?'

'Well – no.' The little man's face fell, and Bansi hurried on. 'I expect you need to speak to Pogo about it.'

'*What?* You haven't entrushted it to *him*, have you? Don't get me wrong, Pogo'sh a fine fellow, but never give a brownie something like that to look after! They're not relia-bia-biable, so they're not!'

'Really, Flooter? Oh, dear. Tell you what, why

don't you go and find Pogo, tell him where I am, and ask him where he's hidden the key?'

Flooter pouted. 'No use asking Pogo for anything. He's Mr Grumpy, so he is.'

'But maybe if you tell him where he can find me, he'll be more helpful.'

Flooter's eyes lit up. 'Ah, now, young lady, that'sh a very very fine plan indeed. A sort of trade. I'm looking for something, and so'sh he . . . Grand! I'll tell Pogo where you are, and he'll give me the key, and I'll look after it for you, sho I will . . .'

Bansi blinked. Flooter had disappeared, and she wasn't sure how; although she'd been looking straight at him, she felt as if she must have glanced away for an instant. She shook her head disbelievingly and gazed around the clearing again, wondering how to occupy her time until Pogo and Tam arrived. If they ever did. The cluricaun didn't seem terribly dependable, but for now trusting him and staying put looked like her only option. Still, the glade was a pleasant place to be; the sunlight was warm and the chirruping of the forest birds was soothing. Standing, she checked the poker; it slid smoothly from her belt. She resolved not to worry; Tam and Pogo would find her sooner or later, and she'd be quite safe until they did.

* * *

Miles away, a great grey wolf paused and sniffed the breeze. It turned its head towards the distant forest, sniffed again, and broke into a run. Behind it, four warriors on horseback followed – three men and a woman, all young and lean and strong and beautiful, with black hair that streamed out behind them like victorious banners. Their faces, white and smooth and lovely, were wickedly set in masks of cruel merriment. In the sunlight, their jagged bronze weapons gleamed sharp and deadly.

Chapter Thirteen

It seemed to Bansi as if she'd been waiting for ever. The sun was climbing higher in the sky, edging its way towards midday; the forest was still and peaceful. There was a distant chirruping of birds and, far off, the sound of a running stream, but in the clearing nothing was moving.

She was bored.

So it was understandable, when she heard the sweet sound of singing moving through the forest, that she decided to investigate.

Keeping close to the trees and walking as silently as she could, Bansi made her careful way towards the sound. It was a beautiful, pure voice, and though she couldn't make out the words it was singing, the melody was gentle and soothing. Something about it seemed almost to be drawing her, calling her, summoning her. She crept closer, following the sound of the song as it moved through the trees, until at last she peered round one great ancient trunk and saw the voice's owner.

It was a young woman – tall, slender and very beautiful. She wore a dress the colour of the sky, and her hair was silky and golden. Over her arm she carried a woven basket. She was moving with delicate grace along a forest track, pausing from time to time to pick mushrooms and wild herbs, singing as she went.

Bansi kept herself pressed out of view against the tree trunk, watching. But the woman had only taken a few steps past the tree where Bansi was hiding when she stopped and looked around.

'Who's there?' she asked. Her voice when she spoke was as clear and lovely as the song had been. 'Who is it?'

Bansi felt a sudden twinge of guilt, as if she had been caught spying.

'Don't be afraid!' the woman continued, as if coaxing a frightened animal. 'I know you're there. I won't hurt you!'

Everything about the way she moved and spoke made Bansi feel sure she was friendly. And it would be nice to have a friend here, someone to talk to while she waited for Pogo and Tam . . .

Almost without coming to a decision, Bansi stepped out from behind the tree. The beautiful woman laughed; a merry, rippling laugh like running water. 'And what kind of elf are you?' she enquired, her eyes twinkling.

'Oh, I'm not an elf,' Bansi began, and then stopped, unsure how much she should say. She had never been fearful of strangers, but her parents had always taught her to be wary, and here in this alien place she thought she should probably be on her guard all the more. On the other hand, how could this gentle lady possibly be dangerous?

As she hesitated, the lady laughed again. She stepped towards Bansi, bringing with her the scent of a gloriously fragrant perfume. Bansi inhaled; the smell was intoxicating, magical. She felt her anxiety begin to drift away. 'I'm not an elf,' she repeated vaguely. 'I'm a girl. A human girl.'

The young woman laughed again. 'I know,' she said. 'I can tell, sweet one. But what are you doing out here all alone? Don't you know these woods are full of danger?'

'I'm . . . I'm waiting for someone. A friend.'

The lady smiled. 'It's good to have friends, isn't it? But I can't leave you here. It isn't safe. Why don't you come home with me, and wait for your friend there?'

Bansi shook her head, which was feeling fuzzier by the minute. 'It's very kind of you, but I mustn't. I need to go back to where he'll expect to find me . . .' Her voice tailed off as the woman stepped forward and took her hands in a tender, friendly gesture.

'Oh, don't refuse my hospitality,' she teased softly. 'A true friend will find you wherever you are!' And then she started humming softly, the same sweet melody she had been singing before, and Bansi somehow felt that she must be right: if Pogo was a true friend he'd know where to find her . . .

'Come with me,' the woman said in an enchanting sing-song voice that somehow carried the tune on, unbroken, and Bansi thought how wonderful that would be, to go wherever this lovely woman took her and to stay with her always . . .

'All right,' she smiled, and allowed herself to be led off, unresisting, deeper into the woods.

Chapter Fourteen

High in the air and far away the swan circled, searching without success.

'It's no good,' Pogo muttered anxiously. 'She could be anywhere. If she's even through the gate yet.'

'Aye, well, you're going the wrong way, you know,' a voice behind him slurred. 'Oh – right way now . . . no, wrong way again . . . right way . . . wrong way . . .'

Pogo turned with a scowl. 'Flooter!' he growled. 'How did you get up here?'

The cluricaun beamed merrily. 'Nobody knowsh how the cluricaun travel,' he observed, tapping his nose, 'not even the cluricaun. Whoopsh!'

Pogo grabbed him just in time.

'Anyhow,' Flooter continued knowingly, 'I've got something to tell you. And then maybe you'll have something to tell me, eh?' He nudged Pogo meaningfully but inaccurately. Once more, Pogo caught him.

'What *are* you on about?' the brownie snarled impatiently, holding the cluricaun's collar tightly in his fist. 'And what did you mean, we're going the wrong way?'

'Ah, very wise, Pogo. Caution, that'sh the way.' A thoughtful look came over him. 'She's awful young to have her own wine cellar, ishn't she? I'd have thought she'd be older.'

One hand still gripping the cluricaun's collar, Pogo scanned the horizon distractedly. 'You'd have thought *who* would be older, you drunken fool?'

Flooter's eyebrows crawled slowly up his forehead. 'Why, Bansi, of courshe. Who elshe have we been talking about?'

'*What?* You've seen her? Flooter, do you mean to tell me you know where she is?'

The little cluricaun sighed exaggeratedly. 'Dear me, Pogo, you're a bit shlow on the old uptake today, aren't you? Aye, she's in the forest. You know, the big dark one, to the north, that'sh filled with all kinds of fearsome beasties . . . Now, about that key . . .'

Pogo tightened his grip on Flooter's collar as the swan wheeled to face north. 'Where in the forest is she? It's a big place.'

'It is that, Pogo; powerful big. I'll tell you, it's sho big a wee girl could get terrible losht in there. It's sho big it wouldn't shurprise me if—'

'So where *is* she, you stupid great fungus?!?'

'Ah now, Pogo, no need to be like that. You'll hurt my feelings, so you will. She'sh in a big clearing near the hunting ground of the Hag of the Dark Glen, that'sh where she is . . .'

Pogo sucked in a huge angry breath. 'The Hag of the Dark Glen, Flooter? You mean you left a mortal child, on her own, in an open space near the hunting ground of a creature that likes to catch mortal children, boil them up in a big pot and eat them? Is that what you're telling me?'

'It is, aye,' Flooter agreed cheerfully. He looked at the scowling, glowering brownie and something seemed to sink in to his addled consciousness. 'Um . . . did I do wrong, Pogo?'

Pogo shook his head angrily and looked hard at the cluricaun. 'I tell you what: if that wee girl ends up in the Hag's pot, I'll boil you up for soup myself.'

'Ah, Pogo, you wouldn't do that, would you . . . ?'

'I would! And I'd do it gladly! Now here's what you're going to do, Flooter me boy: you're going to find Bansi and you're going to keep her safe till we get there!'

'Ah – right you are, Pogo. Find her, keep her safe and then I'll get the key. Got it . . .' And without even Pogo quite being able to see how, he disappeared.

Pogo turned grimly. Ahead of them, in the far distance, he thought he could just make out the edge of the great forest.

'Fast as you can, Tam,' he muttered. 'Fast as you can.'

All the way along the forest path, the young woman held Bansi's hand gently in hers and kept up a merry stream of chatter. Bansi smiled, vaguely thinking how nice this was. She had a nagging feeling at the back of her mind that she was supposed to be meeting someone, but she couldn't for the life of her remember who, or why. Anyway, she was looking forward to seeing her new friend's house.

'It's a delightful little cottage,' her friend was saying. 'When we get there, you can lie down and have a little sleep . . . before it's time to eat.'

And suddenly, Bansi felt that a little sleep would be just what she needed. She yawned, and allowed herself to be led further along.

'Here we are again!' Flooter called cheerily as he tottered at full speed into the clearing. 'Now, what were we here *for*?' he added. His face took on a crafty look. 'Oh, aye . . . the key to the wee girl's wine cellar. And the wee girl is . . . nowhere to be seen. Right. So to get the wine, I need to get the key; to get the key, I need to make Pogo happy; to make Pogo happy, I need to find the wee girl and keep her safe. Right. Here we go, then.' He shot off into the undergrowth, muttering to himself, and vanished.

'There it is!' the young woman said, pointing along the track to a parting in the trees just a little further ahead, where her home stood.

Bansi looked dreamily at the cottage. It was indeed delightful, like something out of a fairy tale; enormous roses grew around the door, and a white picket fence enclosed it. How nice it would be, she thought, to stay there always; to never, ever leave. Again she yawned, looking forward to a peaceful rest in the lovely lady's house, and sleepily she turned her head, thinking how beautiful her new friend looked.

'What should I call you?' she asked drowsily.

The lady smiled. 'Annis will do, if you must call me anything.'

Suddenly, the tranquillity of the morning was broken by an unearthly howling sound which seemed to come from the trees just ahead.

'Who's there?' Annis called. There was no answer but another tortured howl. 'Who's *there*?' she called again. She let go of Bansi's hand and stepped forward.

Bansi's hand fell lazily to her side. It brushed against the poker which still hung from her belt. She blinked; the dreaminess of her mood suddenly evaporated as if a dark heavy cloud had lifted from around her. She rubbed her eyes and dropped her hand to her side again, clutching the cold iron.

Instantly, the view ahead of her changed. Where Annis had stood, young and beautiful, now a wrinkled, twisted old hag leered hideously into the trees. 'Who's there?' she croaked, as another howl came. 'Show yourself!'

Horrified at the transformation, Bansi looked further along the track to the cottage; and what she saw chilled her. It had become a wretched hovel, ramshackle and disgustingly dirty. The pickets of the fence were long white bones.

And no roses grew around the door. Instead, it was framed with human skulls, discoloured horribly with dried blood.

Chapter Fifteen

Hidden in the undergrowth, Flooter chuckled drunkenly to himself and blew again across the neck of the open bottle. The bottle howled like a soul in torment.

'Heh!' he sniggered. 'Cluricaun magic!' He peered at the Hag through the greenery; her sharp old eyes were still searching far above his head. Glancing at Bansi, who was staring in horror, he noticed approvingly that she was clutching the poker.

'That's it, girl,' he murmured. 'That'll break the spell. Now – run!'

But Bansi was rooted to the spot, stunned by the horrific sight ahead.

'Gah! Pixies playing games, no doubt!' Annis snarled to herself. Turning back towards Bansi, she smiled a hideous smile; her long canines and sharp front teeth glinted gruesomely in the sunlight as she held out one wrinkled, claw-like hand. 'Come, dear child,' she grated. 'Come and sleep, before it's time to eat.' A long, blood-red tongue lashed out and licked her withered lips greedily.

Bansi stepped back in disgust and terror, and the Hag's red-veined eyes widened in surprise. They flicked down to Bansi's waist and took in the sight of her hand grasping the iron handle of the poker.

'What's that for, my dear?' she wheedled. 'Not afraid of me, are you? Come – I'm your friend. I'll keep you safe . . .'

Suddenly and with incredible speed for one so hunched and twisted, she rushed at Bansi, talons extended. Bansi's hand came up; the poker slashed at the Hag's face. She screamed and clutched her eyes, bending double with the pain.

Bansi turned and ran for her life. Behind her, she heard Annis's harsh rasping cry: 'Brúid! Fresh meat! Catch it, Brúid! Catch it and I'll share it!'

From deep in the trees somewhere to Bansi's left came an answer, a deep-throated, animal growl: 'Hurrh! Meat?' Then there was the sound of something large and strong crashing through the woods, snapping off branches as it beat its way towards her.

Bansi gripped the poker tightly. She broke from the track and plunged deeper into the forest, her feet pounding the earth. Twigs snapped and dry leaves crackled underfoot. She heard the Hag screaming again, 'After it, Brúid! That way!' The sounds of pursuit grew louder, closer. Her breath caught in her throat; her lungs burned. Her heart hammered against her ribs. Her legs ached. Desperately she ran.

Ahead, something glittered through the trees like a silver ribbon. A stream. Running water. A vague memory came to Bansi. There was *something,* some mythical creature, that couldn't cross running water. What was it? Vampires? Witches? Fairies? Recklessly she raced towards it, ploughing through bracken, through brambles that tore at her feet. She dodged and darted frantically around branches that clawed and snatched as she passed. The stream grew nearer. So did her pursuer. She dared not look round; her imagination filled with horrors at the thought of what might be chasing her.

The stream was fast, wide, but shallow. Water fractured dazzlingly as it splashed up around her feet. She skidded and skittered on the stream-bed pebbles. The ground rose sharply on the other side. Bansi leaned forward instinctively, not letting her pace drop for a moment as she jammed the poker into her belt and began to climb.

She was barely halfway up when she heard the sound she dreaded: the noise of feet splashing heavily across the stream. She clenched her jaw and ran harder, feeling as if her lungs would burst, as if her legs would collapse under her. Something was grunting forcefully and furiously up the slope behind her. She pressed on, forward and upward through the trees, running, scrambling, dodging branches, never looking back, her eyes searching for the summit. The rise grew steeper. On she scrambled, ever upwards. Something stood above her, ahead of her, through the trees: a high, rocky ridge. It gave her a target, something to aim for; she pushed herself onwards. Her breath scorched her throat. Her legs burned. Still she ran.

And then she realized that the rocky ridge at the top was sheer and high. Too high to climb.

She almost gave in then, almost crumpled and fell; but a voice in her head said, *No!* and she fought her despair and kept clambering. The grunting behind her fell a little more distant, as though her pursuer was unused to such terrain, and this gave her heart. She altered her course, stumbling against thick tree trunks, skidding on dead leaves, urgent fear propelling her towards the top. The ridge rose above her like a forbidding wall, the trees its sentries.

But the trees could be allies as well as enemies. With a strength fuelled by terror, she hauled herself into the lowest branches of one that stood by the ridge and began to ascend. Her limbs throbbed and burned stiffly, but she did not surrender to the pain and exhaustion. Up through the thick branches she climbed, until she reached one which overhung the rocky shelf. Only then did she pause, breathing hard through fiery lungs and throat, and look down to see the thing that pursued her.

It was a huge man: tall and stocky, long-limbed and muscular, barrel-chested, with broad, strong shoulders on which sat . . . nothing.

He had no head.

Two huge, repulsive, scaly eyes swivelled in the hollows above his collarbones, independently pivoting, searching, until first one and then the other fixed on her. He leaned back, staring, and Bansi saw with a shudder of revulsion that in the centre of his naked, hairy stomach sat a slobbering mouth full of jagged teeth.

'Meat!' he grunted. 'Come down, meat! Come *down*!' He wrapped his great arms around the trunk and heaved.

Bansi clung tight, terrified the monster would shake her from the tree or even uproot it altogether; but the brute had overestimated himself. The huge plant stood firm. The monster let go and began to pace angrily.

'Come down, meat!' he growled again, fat droplets of saliva slobbering from his wet red mouth. 'Brúid wants you! Brúid is hungry! Annis is hungry! Come down!'

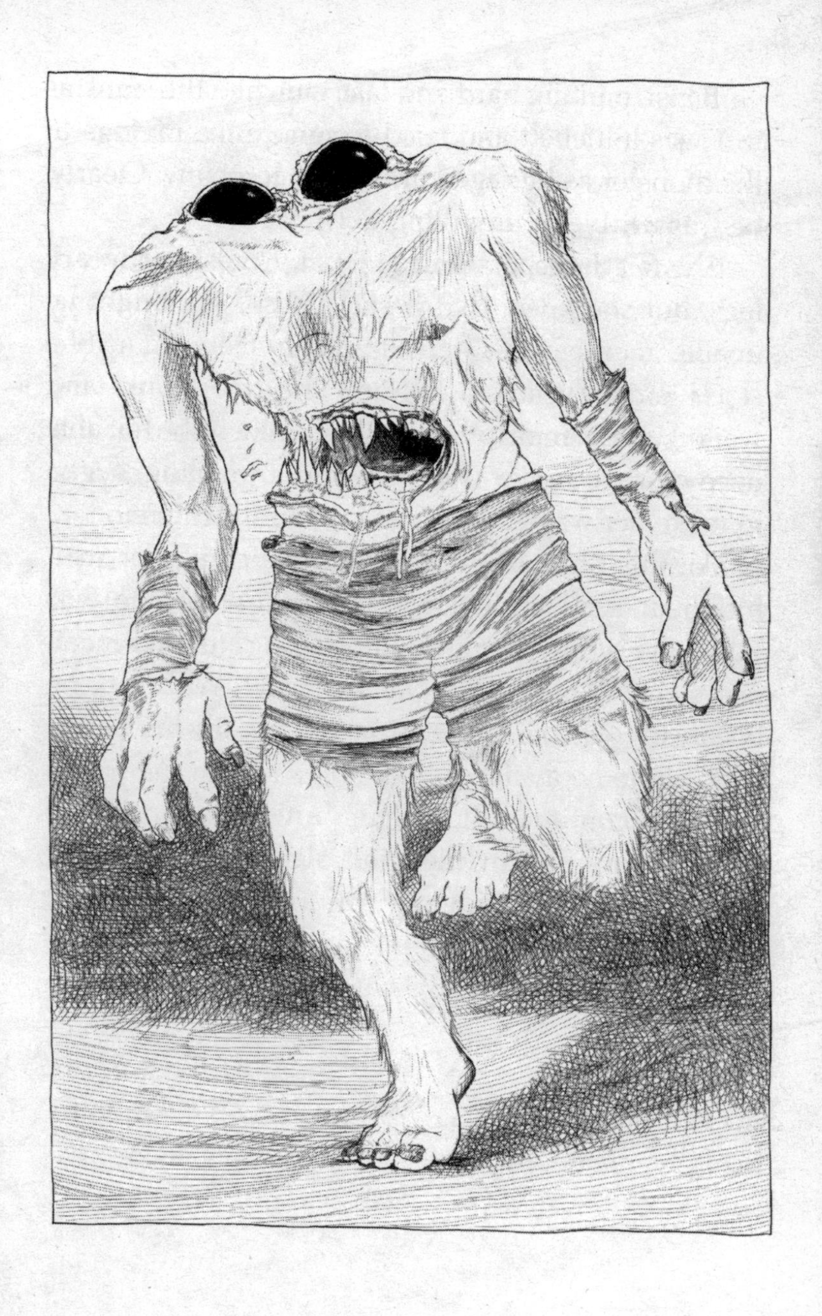

Bansi, panting hard and fast, clutched the trunk as if it was a lifebelt and tried to ignore the ravings of the monster as he raged and stormed below. Clearly, he was unable or unwilling to climb.

She felt a desperate urge to sit, to rest her weary legs; but she knew that if she did so, she might be unable to persuade herself to her feet again. She stood on the branch, holding the tree trunk, and waited until her gasping subsided. When she felt able once more to move, she knelt and, trembling, began to make her way carefully along the sturdy limb.

All this time, Brúid had been watching her with his great scaly rolling eyes. Seeing what she was doing, he set up a renewed howling. 'No! Bad meat! *Bad* meat! Come down! *Not* go away!' With fury he began to kick the tree and strike it with his balled fists, but to no avail.

Bansi continued to edge cautiously along the branch, until she reached the place where it hung over the top of the ridge. It was a short drop to safe ground.

Chapter Sixteen

Bansi could still hear Brúid howling his frustration as she made her way down the slope on the other side of the hill. The trees were sparser here for some reason, and the going was easier. Of course, not being chased by a hungry flesh-eating monster helped, too. But Bansi was cautious now, and kept her poker drawn and ready, just in case.

She had got her breath back by this time, and was determined to put as much distance between herself and Brúid as possible. She kept moving in a straight line away from the ridge, trying not to dwell on the impossibility of the tasks ahead of her: to find Pogo and Tam, and rescue her parents.

She had been walking for some time – an hour or more – when it occurred to her that something was different about this part of the forest. She stopped, puzzled, and looked around; but whatever it was, she couldn't quite work it out. The trees were, as far as she could tell, much the same; so were the ferns and grasses of the forest floor; the birdsong and other animal noises from near and far were still there . . .

It was as she was entering a picturesque glade, with a bright rippling brook running through it, that she realized what it was.

Everything looked clean and unnaturally tidy. No dried, fallen leaves littered the ground. No broken plants, trampled by animals, could be seen. Even the lichen and fungus that grew on and around the trees looked somehow arranged and orderly.

And as she realized this, Bansi began to feel as if something was watching her. She turned slowly, casually, as if regarding the clearing, but her eyes flicked from side to side, looking for signs of life.

She caught a sudden movement, low down, out of the corner of her eye; a flash of brown in her peripheral vision. She spun round, glimpsed something ducking for cover. Something small and, she was sure, man-shaped. Something that could easily have been . . .

'Pogo?' she called hesitantly. 'Pogo, is that you?'

The clearing somehow seemed to fall still for a moment. There was a rustling sound in the bushes, and a noise that sounded like dozens of small voices muttering to each other. She thought she heard the words, '*Pogo! She knows Pogo!*'

Suddenly, the glade was full of brownies. For what seemed like a full minute they stared at her, brown eyes wide and full of reverence. Finally, one stepped forward, cleared his little throat, and asked hesitantly, 'Are – are you the girl he went to find?'

The silence was broken. Bansi was deluged without warning; submerged by an avalanche of excited questions that rolled unstoppably from the eager mouths of the little people.

'Where is he?'

'Why are you alone?'

'Are you going to help us?'

'How did you get here?'

On and on the tide of questions rolled, most of them lost in the swell of chatter, until finally one of them – a little woman in a tattered tunic, her face almost as wrinkled as Pogo's – stepped forward, turned to face her tribe, and held her hands up. Immediately there was silence.

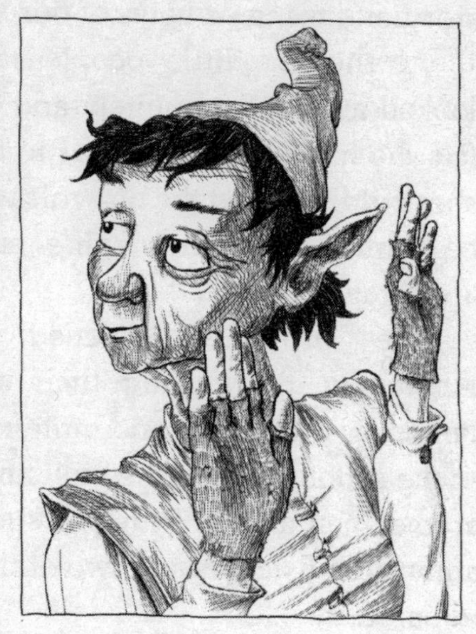

'Give the child a

moment to speak!' she cried. Then, turning to Bansi with a movement that could have been either a stumble or a clumsy half-curtsey, she said, 'Our pardon. But please, tell us – are you the child of the Blood of the Morning Stars?'

Bansi wasn't sure how to answer. 'Well – I suppose so,' she began. 'I mean – Pogo says I am . . .' She got no further before the entire brownie gathering, as one, dropped to one knee – all but the woman who had spoken, who performed her clumsy curtsey once more.

'Then you are most welcome,' the little woman continued, 'and we ask that you would tell us your story, and bring us news of our kinsman Pogo.'

At this the little people sat cross-legged and looked at Bansi so politely and expectantly that she felt she had little choice but to begin. As quickly as she could, she told the brownies of the night's events, beginning with the wolf's sudden and violent appearance.

The brownies listened respectfully and attentively, murmuring their approval each time Pogo was mentioned and muttering dark displeasure at the actions of first the wolf and then the Hag. But at the mention of Brúid, a sudden hubbub arose among her listeners and two or three rose to their feet in panic.

The little woman gestured for silence. After a moment, Bansi continued haltingly, not sure what to make of their reaction; but as she told of how she had made her escape from the monster there was uproar, sudden and overwhelming. Seized by panic, the brownies leaped to their feet and darted pell-mell into the undergrowth. In an instant, no one was left but Bansi and the small brown woman.

'You must go,' the woman said urgently. 'You must leave us now.' Seeing the confusion on Bansi's face, she explained hurriedly. 'The monster you encountered – the Brúid creature – it does not give up. Not once it has seen the face of its prey. It will be here soon.'

Bansi felt her heart collapse in despair. 'But – it couldn't climb the ridge! How will it find me?'

'It will find a way. The ridge does not go on for ever. And if it finds you here, we are not safe. You must go!'

'Go where?' Bansi blinked angrily against the prickle of despairing tears.

The little woman regarded her sorrowfully for a second. Then, without warning, she grabbed hold of the seam of Bansi's jeans and scurried up her body to rest on her shoulder.

'You're but a child,' she said sadly. 'More than this I can't do, but I will see you safely to the borders of our roaming-ground. There are many dangers in Tir na n'Óg, and some of those are worse still than the beast which pursues you. I cannot keep you safe from Brúid, but perhaps I may help you stay alive for long enough to aid your parents. This way! Go!'

Bansi took a deep breath, straightened her back, and began to walk.

Chapter Seventeen

'You may call me Moina,' the brownie woman told Bansi, after they had travelled some distance in silence.

Bansi said nothing.

'Please,' Moina went on, 'you mustn't blame my people. We are small, and powerless. There is nothing any of us can do against the great forces of this land.'

'Pogo doesn't think so,' Bansi answered sharply.

'Pogo is brave,' Moina said. 'But bravery isn't enough.'

'Nor is cowardice.'

Moina sighed. 'Pogo has gone to stand against the Dark Sidhe,' she said, 'but they are strong. They have great magic where we have none. What chance have we against them?'

'Every chance! Good grief, Moina, you can touch iron! You can use it as a weapon!' Even as she said it, Bansi could feel her passenger stiffening with tension.

'No faery ever wields iron against another!'

'Why not?'

'The laws forbid it!'

'And who makes the laws? I mean, I bet they'd use their magic against you!'

'Why wouldn't they? Magic is an honourable weapon!'

'And iron isn't?'

Moina looked shocked at the idea. 'Of course not! Using iron is a mortal trick!'

'So what you're saying is: they make the rules, and they've decided *their* weapons are OK, but *yours* aren't, and you just go along with that. And then you complain about being powerless. That's a bit pathetic, isn't it?'

Moina glowered. 'You wouldn't understand.'

'You're right. I don't understand why you'd let someone else make up a silly rule that means they get to win without even trying.'

Moina's scowl deepened, so that for a moment she looked extraordinarily like Pogo. Then, with an effort, she smiled weakly. 'Let's not argue,' she said. 'I'm afraid you may not have much time left.'

'Leaving aside how tactless that remark was,' Bansi told her firmly, 'perhaps you're wrong. You could fight the Dark Sidhe with iron; you just choose not to. Maybe I've got more hope against Brúid than you imagine.'

Moina shook her head, glumly but silently.

On Bansi trudged. The sun continued its long journey across the sky. They came to another forest stream and followed it. The wood began to thin out. Soon, they came to the top of a grassy slope where the trees were so sparse, it was clear they were at the forest's edge.

'I must leave you here,' Moina said sadly. 'Goodbye, child. You are brave.' She leaned over and brushed Bansi's cheek gently with her wrinkled lips; then she scrambled down from the girl's shoulder. Raising her tiny hand, she pointed in the direction of a distant hill. 'That way lies the Court of the Dark Sidhe. You may find your parents there. Whether at the hands of the Brúid creature or the Dark Lord, I wish you a sudden and painless end.'

'I know you mean well,' Bansi answered, sounding more courageous than she felt, 'but I'm not going to give up and lie down. I don't intend to die today, Moina.' She knelt down and looked the little brownie in the eyes. 'Fight back against the Dark Sidhe,' she said. 'Don't let them bully you. Don't let them have it all their way.'

Moina made no answer, but raised one tiny hand in farewell.

Bansi set off down the slope. At the bottom, she turned to wave once more.

Something felt wrong. Everything looked just as it should, but one of her senses was giving off uneasy signals.

It took her a moment to realize it was her sense of hearing. As they'd walked through the woods, there had been constant birdsong. Now – nothing. No noise. It was too quiet, as if something had disturbed the wildlife, scared it into silence.

The hillside paused. Nothing moved. Time stood still.

Suddenly a bird broke cover, frightened by movement. Bansi shook herself, foreboding filling her. A shape burst from the woods: the shape of a tall, muscular man.

A man with no head.

'Moina!' Bansi yelled. 'Look out!'

Moina needed no warning. She had already turned; seen the creature bearing down on her. She leaped for cover. Brúid ignored her. His hideous scaly eyes were fixed on Bansi. With a horrible slobbering cry of triumph he broke into a run, hurtling down the slope towards her. She looked around; there was no escape. No low branches; nothing to climb. Nowhere to run.

The world grew small. The monster filled her vision; the only sounds she could hear were the thundering of his feet and the rasping of his breath.

Now she could smell him: a stale, acrid stench that filled her nostrils.

Bansi O'Hara raised the poker and prepared to die.

Brúid slowed. He stopped.

'Hurrh!' rumbled the dreadful mouth, the stomach around it rippling gruesomely. 'Meat run. Brúid run faster. Good game. Run now, meat. Run!' The teeth were exposed in a frightful parody of a smile. The creature took a single step closer; and then another. '*Run!*' he demanded.

As the monster lurched towards her, another sound began to intrude upon the narrow world of Bansi's perceptions. Slowly it grew, forcing itself into her consciousness.

It sounded like screaming.

Familiar voices, screaming.

And the roaring of an engine.

Behind Brúid, just uphill, a shadow appeared. It bloomed, blossomed into a familiar shape. Bansi's eyes widened in disbelief. She threw herself sideways. The monster laughed.

'Ha! Run, meat! Brúid catch you!' he taunted. '*Oomph!*' he added as a dark green Morris Minor Traveller, rolling madly side over side, caught him square in the back. It bowled him over, ran him down, pressed him hard into the earth.

On the car tumbled until with a final bounce it came to rest, by some miracle the right way up, at the foot of the slope.

Bansi stared for a moment, heart in mouth. Hesitantly she made her way towards the Morris Minor, half afraid of what she might find inside.

And then the doors popped open and her grandmother and Mrs Mullarkey squeezed out, arguing loudly.

'Oh, my poor head! Your driving will be the *death* of me, Nora, so it will!'

'My driving? I like that, Eileen! There wouldn't have been a problem if you hadn't distracted me with all your yelling and screaming!'

'Oh, so I'm supposed to keep quiet while you kill me, am I?' Granny noticed Brúid, lying still on the hillside above them, and her hand flew to her mouth. 'Nora! You *have* killed someone! You've knocked that poor man's head off! It'll be lying around here somewhere! Oh, I can't look!'

Bansi found her voice, though it trembled a little. 'It's OK, Granny. He didn't have a head to begin with.'

Granny wheeled at the sound of her beloved granddaughter. 'Oh, my wee darling!' she cried.

Bansi ran to her, arms wide, found herself seized in a warm and welcome embrace.

'Thank goodness you're safe, love!' Granny said. She looked down at her, and then her smile changed to a puzzled frown. 'What do you mean, he didn't have a head?'

'Never mind that,' Nora Mullarkey interrupted, bustling over to them. 'Just look what he's done to my car!'

They looked. The Morris Minor Traveller was scratched and battered. The roof was badly dented from the collision with the tree in the stone circle. One window was smashed, and the rear seat was covered in leaves and twigs and a huge broken branch.

'I don't think you can blame that headless fellow for all of that,' Granny pointed out.

'He's one of the Good People, isn't he?' Mrs Mullarkey spat, marching up the hill towards the hollow where the fallen monster lay. 'It's their fault, and they're all as bad as each other.' Bending over the lifeless brute, she examined it with dispassionate curiosity. Bansi felt herself flinch anxiously, even though she was sure the creature was no longer dangerous. 'Oh-ho,' Mrs Mullarkey exclaimed. 'One of *those* beasties. The Anthropophagi, and men whose heads do grow beneath their shoulders. Fancy them being real after all. Well, that'll teach *you* to go terrorizing wee girls. And,' she added to the world in general as she made her way back down the hill towards the distraught-looking Morris Minor, 'he won't go leaving people's cars in this sort of state again, either.'

'I think the way you slammed us against that big tree might have had something to do with it, too,' Granny pointed out. 'If that magic hadn't worked just when it did . . .'

'Yes, well that's because I was *right*, wasn't I? About it still being dawn in the circle, even if the sun had risen on the other side of the hill.'

'Here – there's a point,' Granny interrupted. 'It *was* dawn a minute ago. Now it looks like the middle of the afternoon. How did that happen?'

Mrs Mullarkey tutted impatiently. 'If you knew

anything worth knowing, Eileen, you'd know that time doesn't mean the same to . . . to *them* as it does to us. It's different here. Knowing our luck, by the time we get back home a hundred years'll have gone by, and they'll have stopped both our pensions. In any case,' she added, casting another glance at her miserable-looking car, 'whatever time it is here, I'll bet there's no such thing as an open garage or a decent mechanic.'

'But you can still drive it, can't you?' Bansi put in. 'So if we can find out where they've taken Mum and Dad, maybe we can still reach them in time!' As she said this, she felt hope light up inside her. For the first time since waking in the clearing all those hours ago, she felt that perhaps – just perhaps – they had a chance of success.

'That's true,' Mrs Mullarkey agreed. 'Ah – no, it isn't,' she added, inspecting the vehicle more closely. 'Not for a few minutes, anyway. We've got a flat tyre.'

And so they had. There was nothing to be done but change it. Nora Mullarkey unloaded several heavy cardboard boxes from the boot of the car, and produced the jack and spare tyre from the underfloor compartment.

'Take a look through those,' she told Bansi, with a nod at the boxes. 'It's all the scrap metal your Granny's been hoarding in her garage. It looks promising enough – there's some old horseshoes in there, for one thing. Sort out everything that's made of iron and put it back in the car. Iron,' she repeated meaningfullly. '*Not* steel.'

Bansi set to work. Mrs Mullarkey and Granny turned their attention to the flat tyre, squabbling contentedly about every little detail.

It was as they were jacking the car up that something moved among the foliage on the back seat. Something alive, but not human.

Chapter Eighteen

The creature thrashed furiously, beating the leaves and twigs with angry black wings, struggling for freedom.

They stepped back cautiously. Bansi drew the poker once more. Mrs Mullarkey, eyes fixed on the broken window, dipped her hand into a box of ironware and pulled out a horseshoe. The movement continued, growing wilder, as whatever it was strove to liberate itself.

Suddenly a head emerged through the broken pane – a small black head with a thick, powerful beak. One dark, beady eye regarded them and fixed on Mrs Mullarkey.

'You!' it exploded. 'Oh, bloomin' 'eck, I might have guessed!' With a flick of the head it took them all in again and turned its attention to its surroundings. 'Hang on, where's my tree? Where are the stones? Where . . . Aw, *no*! We're *there*, aren't we? You *stupid* old *bat*! You've gone and done it to me! *No!*'

Infuriated, the raven hopped out through the

broken window and stared up at Mrs Mullarkey. 'You . . . you . . . don't you wave that horseshoe at me, missus, not after what you've just gone and done!'

'What *are* you going on about?' Mrs Mullarkey snapped.

The raven glared. 'All I had to do was stay there, that's all. Just stay there.'

It occurred to Bansi, as she squatted down, that only the day before a talking raven would have been the most amazing thing she had ever seen in her life. Now her sole concern was whose side it was on; but the raven didn't seem dangerous, just furious. 'Stay where?' she asked it. 'What do you mean?'

The raven fixed her with an angry look. 'You don't think I've always looked like this, do you? Once, I was just a simple faery – no need to look like a snake's crawled up your bottom, missus,' it added scornfully, glaring again at Mrs Mullarkey. 'It's all right if *we* say it. Come to that, it's all right if you say it *here*; it's only in your own world that it'll draw us to you.

'Where was I? Oh, yeah. Once, I was just a simple faery – a pixie, as it happens. Only then the Lord of the Dark Sidhe turned me into a raven. Not for ever, mind – just for five hundred years.' It laughed bitterly. 'Five hundred blinking years! And here's the thing: I had to be in that tree in the stone circle every twilight, morning and night – but I had to stay in the mortal world, see? The curse said, if I come back here, the five hundred flipping years start all over again! Easy, I thought. Just stay up in the tree. You have to be touching the earth to pass through the gate. Or if you're touching something else that goes through the gate – sitting on a horse, say – you'll go with it. But you're safe in the tree. Anyway, the gate hardly ever opens these days. So, I think, I'll just stay in the tree, do my time, get turned back and be a bit more careful whose larder I'm raiding next time.

'But then,' it continued, looking resentfully at Mrs Mullarkey, 'along come these two old biddies, bouncing and rolling in their old car. *Bang!* The branch I'm perching on goes through the window and gets torn off! Suddenly I'm in the car, the car's on the ground, and *Wham!* – here I am, back at square one.'

'And . . . how long had you been there?' Bansi asked cautiously.

The bird looked at her. Its throat quivered, as if it was trying to force out words too painful to say. Its head twitched; it looked daggers at Mrs Mullarkey.

'Four hundred and ninety-three years!' it howled suddenly. 'Four hundred and ninety-three years of eating carrion and roadkill! Mostly *her* roadkill, lately! You've no idea how hard it is getting the gooey bits out of a hedgehog that's been flattened the way *she* flattens 'em. It's bearable,' he sniffed, 'when you know it's not for much longer. When you know it's only for seven years more ... *but not for another blinking five hundred! I can't stand it!*'

Bansi and Granny stared awkwardly at each other, not knowing what to say. But Mrs Mullarkey was not abashed.

'Hmmmph!' she snorted. 'Well, all I can say is that no one asked you to go breaking and entering my car!'

The raven stared, open-beaked, and for a moment Bansi was afraid it was going to do Mrs Mullarkey some damage.

'But now that you're here,' the old lady went on, 'perhaps you can help us, and help yourself into the bargain.'

'Help you!' the raven spluttered.

'That's right. We're here to stop the Dark Sidhe killing my friend's young granddaughter, here, and her parents as well. And perhaps when we do that, we can persuade him to undo the spell on you. How does that sound?'

The raven's beak dropped open in surprise. After a moment, it closed it again with a sharp *clack!* 'It sounds completely bonkers,' it said. 'Count me out. This is what he did to me when I just got up his nose a bit. Imagine what he'd do if he got really cross!' It spread its wings and took to the air. Within moments, it was just a small black speck against the sky. Bansi watched it go, a twinge of pity tugging at her heart.

'Well! Talk about unreasonable!' Mrs Mullarkey tutted.

About ten minutes later, the raven was sitting at the top of a tree in the forest, muttering to itself, when a movement far above caught its eye. Wary of predators, it spread its wings once more in readiness for flight as it looked up.

It was a swan, and it was closing in rapidly. Within moments it was circling within shouting distance.

'Hey!' the brownie on its back yelled down. 'Have you seen a mortal child near here?'

The raven hunched its shoulders in an all-the-world's-against-me kind of gesture. 'Might've done,' it said peevishly.

Pogo scowled. 'Never mind "might",' he said. 'Have you seen her or not?'

'All right, then, I have. What's your point?'

'The point is, either you tell us where she is or my friend here will turn into a great big eagle and eat you.'

The raven eyed the swan warily. There was something very unswanlike about its expression just at that moment. 'She's at the edge of the forest, with two barmy old ladies. Or she was a few minutes ago.'

Pogo was so relieved he almost smiled. 'Well, now,' he said, 'at last something goes right. Whereabouts at the forest's edge?'

The raven indicated with its beak. 'About where that wolf and those four armed warriors are heading.' It looked back at Pogo and Tam – but they were no longer there. They were just a blur, shooting towards the edge of the forest.

'Oh, no,' the raven called sulkily after them, 'don't bother saying "thank you" or anything! Don't bloomin' mention it! Don't mind me! Nobody else does!' It sighed. 'Don't even know where my next bit of roadkill's coming from. Who'd be a raven, eh?'

Chapter Nineteen

It began with hoofbeats, thundering like drums. Bansi turned. The horses were already upon them. An arm reached down to grab her. She lashed out, struck it with cold iron. The warrior recoiled with a yell of pain and anger. Even as his speed carried him on, the second rider bore down. Bansi whirled, swinging the poker. The horse started away. The wolf sprang from nowhere, all teeth and claws; her forearm was caught, seized agonizingly in its powerful jaws. Bansi cried out; the weapon fell from her grasp. The third horseman leaned down and swept her in one single fluid motion onto his horse's back.

Mrs Mullarkey screamed fury and hurled her horseshoe. It struck Bansi's captor hard. He flinched, but did not fall. The fourth horseman grabbed the old woman by the hair. She yelled in pain. There was a nauseating blur of enchantment as she, too, was lifted onto horseback and carried away.

It had taken seconds. Granny, hidden from view as she knelt, jacking up the car, had no time to react before it was over. She leaped to her feet, hurled useless threats and curses at the departing backs of the kidnappers; but within moments they had passed out of sight. She was alone.

Or so she thought. She was unaware of the hidden eyes that watched her. From the shelter of a gnarled old tree at the top of the slope, Moina looked on, her thoughts in turmoil. And in a tall clump of wild grass nearby, a little cluricaun bit his lip in dismay.

In the undergrowth at the forest's edge, other eyes watched, too.

The world whirled by; the tall trees at the forest's edge were no more than a continuous blur of browns and greens. Bansi struggled with her captor against the firm grip that held her tight; the studs and ridges of his ornate leather breastplate dug painfully into her back. She yelled; she jerked and thrashed; she screamed; and when the warrior clamped one hand over her mouth, scraping her cheek roughly with the knotted thong that fastened his wristband, she bit down hard. The man cursed violently. Seconds later, she felt a sharp sting against her neck. She froze as he drew the knife blade lightly around her throat and tweaked her ear lobe with it; a warm, wet droplet welled up beneath its touch.

'A sacrifice without ears,' the man hissed, softly

and darkly, 'is still a sacrifice.' Bansi flinched. She felt the point press and ease, press and ease with the smooth galloping motion.

Without warning, the horse came to a halt. Bansi dared not move her head; but she rolled her eyes downwards to see the wolf standing in front of them, teeth bared in a silent snarl. The other horses had stopped, too, forming a crescent around the great grey beast, their riders grinning, leaning forward in anticipation of an entertaining quarrel. Bansi's captor slowly relaxed his grip on her; she felt the pinprick of the knife point withdraw.

The wolf shrugged off its pelt, letting it fall to the ground, and Conn stood there, his face cold and hard. 'Put the dagger away, Kearn. The child is not to be harmed. Not *yet*, and not by us.'

'The Lord said nothing of that,' the warrior answered dismissively.

Conn glowered. '*I'm* saying something of it. Not one drop of her blood is to be spilled. Or you answer to me.'

Bansi couldn't see the man's face, but she heard the amused contempt in his reply. 'Aye, well, it's a shame you didn't mention it earlier.' He held up his knife in front of her, almost touching her face; a blurred trickle of blood ran down its shining bronze blade. 'I've already spilled a drop.'

Conn's face betrayed nothing. 'Then you answer to me,' he said, in a voice at once calm, controlled and deadly.

Instantly, with perfect, gymnastic grace, Kearn was off the horse. He towered over Conn, his stance relaxed, confident, threatening, and looked down at him with an expression Bansi recognized from the playground. It was the smile of a bully showing off to his gang, ready to play cat with a new victim.

'Now, boy?' he asked, flashing a white-toothed film-star grin. With a single, swift movement, one long lean leg hooked the wolfskin and brought it backwards, out of Conn's reach. 'Without your dressing-up clothes? And with no weapons?' He brandished his dagger mockingly. 'If you wish. The Dark Lord'll be sorry to lose you, I'm sure, but my bringing the child to him will more than make up for that.'

Bansi's gaze darted cautiously from one face to the next. Kearn's eyes and Conn's were locked together, shutting out all else. The other warriors were entirely focused on them, hungry now for the scent of blood. The one who held Mrs Mullarkey was enraptured, his smile wide and greedy in cruel anticipation; the other horseman's pale, beautiful face was flushing with excitement; the woman was licking her red lips as if to taste the wounds of battle, her gleeful eyes fixed on the combatants. They pressed in, unconsciously nudging their horses closer, edging Bansi out. Her horse stepped back; she tugged the rein, dug her heels into the horse's sides as unobtrusively as she could, willing it to turn and run.

There was no response; not even a twitch. She tried again, harder. The horse ignored her.

She looked around again and met Mrs Mullarkey's gaze. Her granny's friend was still held fast by her captor, but her eyes fixed on Bansi's, held her and then flicked towards the forest. Again they fixed on her, held and flicked. The message was unmistakable.

Go.

Her first thought was that she couldn't leave Mrs Mullarkey to the mercies of these cruel faery warriors. But this was not just about her. It was about her parents; it was about Pogo, and Tam, and the lives of who knew how many others like them; it was about making sure a cruel tyrant did not gain power. And with a stab of fear that made her shudder, a line from the prophecy returned to her:

Then shall the ways between the worlds reopen.

Would the Dark Lord be satisfied with ruling only Tir na n'Óg if he could bring his evil to the mortal world? It didn't bear thinking about. She looked again at Mrs Mullarkey, who was staring at her with urgent eyes, and her mind was made up.

No one else was watching. The other horses were edging forward, crowding in; their riders leaned forward intently. Conn and Kearn were fixed on each other, the rest of the world shrunk to shadows for both of them.

She moved one leg quietly across the horse's back.

'Come on, then, boy,' the warrior said, scorn edging his tone. 'Time to make me answer to you. If you can do it without your hearthrug.'

Conn breathed deeply, his whole body relaxing. 'You know, Kearn,' he said calmly, 'the wolf isn't all in the skin.'

The sudden, sheer animal savagery of the attack was frightening. He leaped, catching Kearn off-balance, knocking his knife-arm aside, bringing him down like a wounded deer. His teeth tore at the man's throat. There was a ghastly gurgling sound.

Bansi slipped off the horse and ran. The ground was more level here, and they were still close to the forest's edge. It took her only moments to reach it.

And it took only moments for Kearn's body to stop twitching.

Conn stood, his mouth smeared with blood, and scooped up his wolfskin cloak, fastening it round his neck. He glanced at the riderless horse, glared fury at his companions, and cocked his head for a moment as if listening. Then he bent and picked up Kearn's dagger. Holding it to his nose, he sniffed the drop of blood at its tip.

Bansi ran, keeping the broadest trees between her and the enemy. Her mind raced; she tried desperately to think of a way of rescuing Mrs Mullarkey, of finding help, of re-arming. She could think of nothing.

She twisted and weaved as she ran, trying to make her trail as hard as possible to follow, running as lightly as she could, constantly checking for signs of pursuit.

Conn stepped out in front of her.

She swerved, changed course, tried to dive for cover behind a tree, but he was much too fast. A moment later he had her. His grip was like a steel claw.

'That,' he said softly, 'was stupid. I have the scent of your blood in my nostrils. I can track you down anywhere, wherever you go. I can run behind you, and you will not hear me. I can hunt you down, and you will not see me. I am swifter and more deadly than any mortal. You cannot escape me. If you try, I will kill the old woman. Very slowly. And I will make you watch.' He grinned cruelly. His teeth were still red with Kearn's blood.

Bansi shuddered, and did not resist as he led her back to the horses. She tried not to look at Kearn's body as Conn mounted the fallen warrior's horse and hauled her up to sit in front of him.

'I'll repeat this,' the boy told the remaining three warriors, who looked at him with a new, fear-tinged respect. 'The girl is not yet to be harmed in any way. We'll bring her to Balor's Hollow unmarked. If she causes us any more trouble,' he added coldly, 'kill the old woman immediately.'

As he dug his heels in to spur the horse on, a

commotion in the nearest tree made him turn his head; but it was nothing. Nothing but a solitary raven taking flight, its wings beating the air noisily.

At the sound of further hoofbeats approaching, Granny turned to run – and stopped as she recognized the huge black horse that had carried Bansi from her home the night before. Its small brown rider was clearly visible between its shoulders. Furious, she stalked towards them, meeting them as they drew up.

'You!' she spat. 'This is all your fault! If you hadn't brought my wee Bansi to this terrible place—'

'Where is she?' Pogo interrupted.

'Gone! Four riders on horses and that wolf creature came and took her, and Nora too! Come on, get me up on that horse with you and we'll get after them!'

Pogo shook his head. 'It's not that simple.'

'Not that simple? They went that way! Just follow the tracks . . .' Her voice tailed off as she looked at the ground where she was pointing. There *were* no tracks. The hoof prints which should have been clearly visible simply weren't there.

'Faery steeds,' Pogo said. 'They leave no hoof prints, save when they choose to. Did they say where they were taking her?'

There was a sudden flurry of wings. 'Balor's Hollow!' announced the raven excitedly, dropping down between them. 'I heard them! They said they were going to Balor's Hollow!'

Pogo eyed the bird suspiciously. 'Are you sure? When did you hear them?'

'Of course I'm flipping sure!' the bird croaked indignantly. 'You don't forget that name in a hurry, do you? I heard them just now, a few miles that way. The little girl escaped, see, and that bloke who turns into a wolf caught her and said they were going to Balor's Hollow! None of my business, I know, but I thought you'd—'

As the horse turned, Granny reached up and caught its mane; with a blur of magic she was on its back, behind Pogo.

Tam accelerated so suddenly that none of them even heard the raven squawking: 'Good manners cost nothing, you know! I mean, that's *twice* now!'

'What did it mean, "you don't forget that name in a hurry"? What's so special about this place?' Granny asked, raising her voice over the rushing of the wind and the pounding of hooves.

'Balor's Hollow,' Pogo told her grimly, 'is one of the three hundred and sixty-six sacred places of Tir na n'Óg. It's also one of the darkest. It lies in permanent shadow, a hollow at the bottom of a crack in the mountains, sitting between cliffs so high and steep that the sun's light can never reach in. Strange things are said to live there – if "live" is the right word.' He shuddered.

'Cheerful wee fellow, aren't you?' Granny observed, trying to ignore the swell of foreboding that rose inside her. She shifted position in an attempt to make herself more comfortable. In doing so, she became aware of something hard and heavy lying across her lap, and a cramp in the fingers of her left hand as if they were gripping something tightly.

It was only as she looked down that she realized she was still holding the jack handle, clutching it like a cold steely lifeline.

Chapter Twenty

It seemed to Bansi that the hooves had been pounding for hours. The same pulse, the same rhythm, the same relentless movement: a mesmerizing tattoo beating its way persistently into her mind. Time seemed to lose all meaning. And still the sun continued its inexorable progress across the sky – moving without compromise towards dusk, the dying of the light, and a nightfall she might not live to see.

As late afternoon turned to early evening, she began to feel as though she was at once sleeping and waking, as if the sound of galloping had somehow entered her bones and become part of her. She began to imagine she could hear drums playing underneath the insistent beating, filling it out, making the whole world echo and throb.

And then it occurred to her that she *could* hear drumming – a cold, deep sound that synchronized seamlessly with the rhythm of the hoofbeats. She shook her head, tried to clear it, reached automatically for her belt before she remembered that she no longer had the poker. The drumming was getting louder now, reverberating through the long narrow valley down which they were galloping; and a sickly feeling of enchantment was growing around her, like the dull dreaminess of the Hag's magic turned sour and nauseating. She clenched her teeth, fought against it. With an effort, she pressed it away, held it off her. She glanced to her left; she could see the strain on Mrs Mullarkey's face as she, too, fought against the poisonous spell.

Ahead of them, the valley narrowed into a pass barely wide enough for a single horse and rider. They pressed onward, increasing their speed. The unseen drummers matched their pace.

They pushed through the pass into Balor's Hollow.

It was a cold, dark, desolate place, enclosed by a jagged cliff face which curved lazily and almost completely around them and was broken only by the narrow pass through which they had entered. High above, it leaned inwards, jutting crags and rocky ledges creating a permanent twilight under which nothing grew save a few twisted, misshapen, stunted specimens of pale and weak plant life. It was as though they were entering an enormous mountain which had been split in two and whose very heart had been torn out, leaving in its place a vast and empty circular arena, its walls dotted with sinister caves and tunnels. The floor of the great basin had once been a single smooth granite slab, but the centuries had cracked and crazed it into an uneven patchwork of jagged rock held together with wide ragged seams of earth. There was something horribly otherworldly about it, like some corrupt and unnatural lunar landscape. At the Hollow's shadowy centre a ring of tall smooth standing stones formed a forbidding circle, like inhuman soldiers standing guard – waiting, Bansi somehow felt apprehensively, for her.

As the horses galloped towards the stone circle, a wild cheering broke out. It echoed around Balor's Hollow above even the sound of the relentless drumming. Bansi cast about, still fighting the dizzy haze of enchantment, but the Hollow seemed empty of anyone else. As they reached the circle Conn urged the horse on, the pounding of the drums accelerating with them as they raced round the perimeter, and as they did Bansi looked up and saw the source of the noises.

In front of a high tunnel near to the pass a large rocky ledge jutted out, forming a natural gallery above the arena. This gallery was crowded with figures, lean and angular and graceful like the warriors, but dressed in clothing altogether richer. They were leaping and dancing around two enormous drums, and somehow Bansi knew they were creating the intense, mind-numbing enchantment that hung in the air like the long moment before the storm breaks. Several of them were beating out the remorseless rhythm as they danced, and all of them were cheering and whooping triumphantly. And as they danced and drummed and cheered, every eye was fixed on her. Absurdly, she found herself thinking of the time she'd been targeted by a gang of bullies at school, drawing strength even now from the memory of how she'd refused to let them crush her. Forcing herself to sit up tall, she glared defiantly up at them.

Conn brought his horse expertly to a standstill just outside the circle. As one, the dancers slowed, the rhythm of the drumming changing to a quiet but insistent double pulse, like the beating of a gigantic heart. Slipping from the horse's back, the wolf-boy held out his hand and motioned to Bansi to follow him down. She dismounted, shrugging him away, and stepped alone with dignity into the circle. Vaguely, she was aware of Mrs Mullarkey being shoved into the circle behind her. She wondered where her parents were, and whether they would be brought here to watch or – she shuddered at the thought – whether they had already been deemed expendable.

'Well,' said Mrs Mullarkey grimly, 'this is a fine to-do, isn't it? We may not get out of this alive. Still,' she went on, brightening, 'at least I got to prove your grandma wrong, eh? All our lives she's been telling me I'm full of old nonsense about the faery folk.' She lowered her voice and went on in a whisper. 'Here – see that tunnel over there? Looks like daylight at the back of it. If I created a diversion, you could run.'

Bansi shook her head. 'They'd kill you.'

'They'll kill me anyway.'

Before Bansi could respond, the tunnel mouth Mrs Mullarkey had indicated flared with light. There was a wailing, uneasily musical sound – some kind of eerie fanfare – and the drums on the stone balcony fell silent. A tall figure strode out, his cloak billowing majestically behind him. Six armed torchbearers – three men, three women, all warriors like Conn's companions – flanked him. The dancers gave a great shout of triumphant welcome, and he paused on the edge of the ring of standing stones to acknowledge them with an arrogant smile. The torchbearers thrust the long shafts of their blazing brands into the cracked floor, where their yellow light blazed with an unnatural intensity; then they withdrew to join Conn had been torn out, leaving in its place a vast and empty circular arena, its walls dotted with sinister caves and tunnels. The floor of the great basin had once been a single smooth granite slab, but the centuries had cracked and crazed it into an uneven patchwork of jagged rock held together with wide ragged seams of earth. There was something horribly otherworldly about it, like some corrupt and unnatural lunar landscape. At the Hollow's shadowy centre a ring of tall smooth standing stones formed a forbidding circle, like inhuman soldiers standing guard – waiting, Bansi somehow felt apprehensively, for her.

As the horses galloped towards the stone circle, a wild cheering broke out. It echoed around Balor's Hollow above even the sound of the relentless drumming. Bansi cast about, still fighting the dizzy haze of enchantment, but the Hollow seemed empty of anyone else. As they reached the circle Conn urged the horse on, the pounding of the drums accelerating with them as they raced round the perimeter, and as they did Bansi looked up and saw the source of the noises.

In front of a high tunnel near to the pass a large rocky ledge jutted out, forming a natural gallery above the arena. This gallery was crowded with figures, lean and angular and graceful like the

warrio
They
enorm
were c
ment tha
the storm
the remors
them were
And as they
every eye was
self thinking o
gang of bullies at
from the memory
crush her. Forcing
defiantly up at them.

Conn brought his
just outside the circle. A
rhythm of the drummi
insistent double pulse, li
heart. Slipping from the h
held out his hand and mot
him down. She dismounted,
and stepped alone with di
Vaguely, she was aware of M
shoved into the circle behind
where her parents were, and whe
brought here to watch or – she

and the three other warriors at a respectful distance beneath the rocky gallery.

The cloaked man stepped alone into the stone circle. He turned to stare at Bansi, and she found herself looking for the first time into the face of the Lord of the Dark Sidhe. Despite his extraordinary thinness he was almost impossibly handsome, but his unlined, ageless face hinted at a capacity for great cruelty and he looked at her as if she was a mere thing. His eyes, which should have been beautiful, shone yellow and hungry like a snake's. With a lithe, predatory movement he came towards her, like a tiger advancing on its prey. She backed away as he approached, keeping her eyes on his, searching for any sign that he was about to pounce. Instead, as he reached the centre of the circle he closed his eyes, raised his face skywards, and howled – a dark, intense, unnatural noise, like the untamed wind of a midnight storm.

And the wind answered. Through the tunnels and the caves of Balor's Hollow came a wild rushing and shrieking that blasted and buffeted all in its way. Bansi fought to stay upright as she and Mrs Mullarkey clung onto one another; but the Lord of the Dark Sidhe, his black hair and cloak streaming out behind him, his expression one of violent ecstasy, spread his arms wide to welcome the tempest.

There was a crack as of thunder; a wave of

uncertain light rolled out from the core of the Dark Lord's being; brightness flared between the standing stones. For a moment the circle was bounded by a wall of magical energy, almost solid in its intensity.

Then there was nothing. No sound. The wind was still; the storm was gone.

As Bansi gasped for breath, the new silence was broken by a harsh slapping sound. Mrs Mullarkey was clapping, slowly and sarcastically. 'That was very dramatic, I must say,' she observed. 'What do you do for an encore? Oh, yes – I remember now. Murder people.'

The Dark Lord glanced at her disdainfully. 'In my kingdom, old hag, there is no law forbidding murder. Or, at least, no law forbidding *me* to murder, which is the important thing. Not that it counts as murder to further shorten the brief life of a mortal, in any case.' His cold gaze fell on Bansi, stabbing through her like an icicle. 'So this is what the bloodlines of the Morning Stars have come to,' he murmured. 'Hardly a worthy vessel. Still, no matter.' He raised his voice and addressed the watchers on the high ledge. 'Ladies and gentlemen, I have brought you here to witness my moment of triumph either because you are my most loyal and faithful followers, or because I want you where I can keep an eye on you. I'm sure you can work out which applies in your own case. In a few moments, I will kill the mortal child and spill the Blood of the Morning Stars onto the sacred earth of Tir na n'Óg. The inheritance of Derga will be mine, and the realm of Faery will be united under my rule. So if any of you *are* planning some little act of treachery, now is your last chance.' He looked at his followers. 'No one? Very wise. I shall remember that. Now, child,' he went on, turning again to Bansi. 'The sun is setting. Time to die.'

From the folds of his robe he drew the white knife. Close to, it was clearly carved from bone; its smooth blade was covered in intricate and unpleasant symbols. His eyes locked with Bansi's; their yellow irises flared. It was like looking into the eyes of a deadly serpent. The weapon rose, ready to strike.

'Run, Bansi!' Mrs Mullarkey cried out suddenly. 'Run!' She hurled herself desperately and furiously against the Dark Lord, grabbing for the knife. 'Run!' she cried again.

Bansi ran.

With a sudden snake-like speed his hand shot out, grabbing Bansi painfully by the throat and dragging her close. He smiled again – a chilling, victorious smile – and lifted the knife. The white blade gleamed evilly.

As he raised it, she saw his head suddenly outlined with light – a coruscating halo of brightness and undulating colour. The air seemed to sparkle and crackle with dark magical scents of incense and bitter cinnamon. The halo flared brighter; a bolt of blue energy leaped with a sharp *crack!* across the gap behind the Dark Lord.

Then there was a dull thud, his grip slackened, his eyes crossed, and he fell over.

Behind him stood Granny O'Hara, framed between the standing stones like a little old avenging angel, the Morris Minor's jack handle her flaming sword. Bansi's heart leaped to see her. On her shoulder Pogo perched, his face wild with fury and triumph.

'Steel!' she yelled, brandishing the jack handle jubilantly; bright sparks of magic flashed around it again as it cut through the unseen barrier. 'Steel! Not iron! See that, Nora I-know-all-about-fairies Mullarkey? My wee Bansi was right! And *you* were *wrong*!'

Of the shocked onlookers on the other side of the circle, Conn was the first to react. With a growl of rage he erupted from his place.

Too late. Already Granny was pushing herself through the invisible barrier, waves of light surging around her, magical energy sparking across the gap from stone to stone. By the time he reached the spot, she was through. He threw himself at the barrier; but in vain.

Pogo leaped down and hurried to Bansi as, in front of Granny, the Lord of the Dark Sidhe staggered to his feet. His eyes blazed with pain and fury; he reached out one hand towards her, muttering some incantation; the other hand gripped the bone-white knife, raised it to strike . . .

Granny hit him with the jack handle again.

And again.

And again.

He stumbled against the barrier. Mystical energy crackled around him; the air filled with the hot smell of dark magic under attack from cold steel. Again Granny struck, and again, relentless, a tiger defending her cub, and with each blow the Lord of the Dark Sidhe was pushed further through the barrier, staggering under the weight of her attack, kept off-balance until for a moment he was trapped entirely within it, like a fly in amber. A final blow; the barrier gave way and he fell through, clutching his head in agony.

Conn howled in fury, seeing his master so abused. He yelled with rage; hurled himself uselessly at the space between the stones; was repulsed.

Granny hugged Bansi close, surrounding her with her warm reassuring scent and, just for a moment, a feeling of safety.

'Excitable wee fellow, isn't he?' she remarked, looking at Conn over Bansi's head. 'Friend of yours?'

'Not exactly,' Bansi told her. 'Remember the wolf that broke your window?'

'And left the room in such a terrible mess,' Pogo added with feeling, from down by Bansi's feet. He was still standing as if to protect her, and though in truth he could have protected not much more than her shins, Bansi was grateful to have him there.

Granny raised an eyebrow. 'This is what he looks

like when he's not being a big doggy, then? That makes sense. I had a dog once; he used to behave just like this at the kitchen door when he wanted walkies.' She looked Conn in the eye. 'Sit!' she commanded. 'Sit!' Conn growled angrily. 'Lie down! Roll over!'

The wolf-boy howled once more, a wordless cry of inexpressible fury. He glared at Granny with pure, raw hatred in his face and flung himself against the barrier again.

'Not very well trained, is he?' Granny observed. 'Let's hope he's housebroken. They can leave great big puddles all over the carpet when they get this excited. What's Nora doing? Has she been taking mime classes?'

Mrs Mullarkey was pushing against her own invisible barrier, unable to move in any direction.

'Yes, very funny, Eileen,' she snapped. 'Now stop practising your comedy routines and get me out of here!'

'Manners, Nora! What's the magic word?'

Mrs Mullarkey scowled. 'If I knew the magic word, I wouldn't need your help, would I?' she muttered. 'Daft old haddock.'

Granny chuckled dryly as she touched the invisible cage with the jack handle. There was a whisper like swishing grass, a strong smell of burning spices, and Mrs Mullarkey was free.

Or as free as one can be, trapped inside an enchanted circle and surrounded by malignant faery people. For the nine sidhe warriors had silently fanned out to take up positions on the boundary of the stone circle. And the Dark Lord himself was rising once more, with murder in his eyes.

Chapter Twenty-Two

Bansi and the others instinctively gathered together, back to back, in the centre of the circle.

'He said no one could get through the barrier,' Bansi said quietly.

'He'll find a way,' Pogo told her grimly. 'It's powerful magic he's created, all right, but he won't have left himself without a way to undo it.'

'If only Tam was here,' Bansi murmured.

'That young lad who changes into horses and things? He brought us here,' Granny said. 'But he can't touch steel,' she went on, with a sideways look at her friend, 'so he couldn't come through that invisible wall thing with us.'

'He'll still be nearby, then!' Bansi exclaimed, hope leaping inside her at the thought. 'If we could just get to him . . .'

'And if he could find some way of bringing all my old iron bits and pieces,' Granny added.

'Aye,' Mrs Mullarkey pointed out sourly, 'and if we could all fly out of here we'd be fine. Well, I'm not going to just stand here wishing for wings. Give me that thing!' she ordered, turning to Granny and snatching the jack handle. 'Right!' she declared, walking forward to address the Dark Lord. 'Seems to me we've got something of a stalemate. So I propose a challenge, Mr Faery. You against me. My weapon' – here she hefted the jack handle threateningly – 'against your magic. The winner walks out of here, free to go, with their entire company.'

Bansi stiffened. 'Is that a good idea?' she whispered to Pogo, kneeling.

'Probably not,' the brownie muttered. 'But I don't have a better one. Only – if he accepts, don't trust anything he says.'

The warriors of the Dark Sidhe smiled mockingly. One of the women drew a long slim dagger and toyed with it, staring contemptuously at Mrs Mullarkey all the while. From the stone gallery above came catcalls and jeers; some of the watching nobility sat down idly, their legs dangling over the edge, as if ready to be entertained.

'I have a better idea,' the Dark Lord said, stepping closer to the barrier, his voice soft as a knife through silk. Bansi found herself shuddering at the sound. 'Surrender, and I'll cut your tongues out and keep you as slaves. Except the girl, obviously.

Believe me, the alternative will be much more unpleasant.'

Mrs Mullarkey looked defiantly back at him. 'That's very big talk. But it seems to me that if you had a way of getting in here, you'd have done it by now.'

The Lord of the Dark Sidhe fixed her with bright, unblinking yellow eyes. 'And you have a means of escape?' His gaze held her, like a snake transfixing its prey before swallowing it whole. 'No? Then choose, old woman. Come out now, and I will be merciful. The girl will die quickly; you, your friend and the brownie will lose your tongues and be pressed into my service.

'Or you can choose to wait in there, while I slowly unweave the enchantment that separates us. In which case, I will spill the girl's blood drop by painful drop. Her screams will be the last sound you hear before I stop your ears. Her dying spasms will be your final sight before I cut out your eyes. And when the sacrifice is complete and the power promised by the prophecy is mine, I will transform you into living statues – blind, deaf, immobile, but fully aware and in constant pain.'

His voice was becoming hypnotic, like the constant murmuring of rainfall on a glass roof. An awful crawling sensation spread over Bansi's skin as she listened, as if a million little spiders were gently spinning their webs over her body. She shivered as though to cast them off and looked at Mrs Mullarkey. The old woman was beginning to sag, weighed down by invisible forces; the Dark Lord's words were clearly wearing down her mental defences.

With an effort, Bansi called out, 'Mrs Mullarkey!' She meant to shout, but the words came out half-whispered, almost like a bad dream where your voice refuses to work.

It was enough. Mrs Mullarkey shook herself. She clutched the jack handle tighter; looked away from those burning yellow eyes; swung her weapon towards him. Sparks burned bright and the air was singed with the hot dark spicy smell of raw magic as the jack handle seared through the barrier towards the Dark Lord's jaw; but this time he was ready. It passed through empty air as he stepped back, effortlessly scornful in his arrogance.

Mrs Mullarkey shook her head again, as if to clear it, and glared at the Dark Lord. 'Well, it's been nice talking to you, young man, but no doubt you have some wee furry creatures to torture, or something of the kind. Don't let me keep you.'

As she turned away, Conn sidled obsequiously up to his master and whispered conspiratorially. The Lord of the Dark Sidhe raised a quizzical eyebrow and inclined his head with studied graciousness.

'Wait!' the wolf-boy commanded, stepping up to the invisible barrier, his eyes fixed on Mrs Mullarkey. The old woman ignored him and kept walking. 'Stop! Come here, Nora Maura Margaret Mullarkey!'

Mrs Mullarkey turned slowly, a strange look in her eyes.

Beside her, Bansi felt Pogo freeze. Instantly, she knew what was happening. 'No!' she yelled. 'Mrs Mullarkey! Block your ears! Don't listen! Mrs Mullarkey! He's trying to enchant you!'

'Come here, Nora Maura Margaret Mullarkey.' Conn repeated, his voice full of malice, and Mrs Mullarkey, jack handle in hand, stepped towards him.

The barrier wreathed her in coruscating fire as she entered it.

Chapter Twenty-Three

'No!' Bansi cried again. 'Mrs Mullarkey! It's an enchantment! Fight against it!' She raced towards the old woman, thinking perhaps to tackle her, to drag her back to safety. Before she could reach her she felt the magical force of the barrier pushing her away as it flowed like a river around Mrs Mullarkey.

Conn seemed to feel it, too; he stepped back, a gloating expression on his face.

He almost didn't see the jack handle scything towards him.

With a yelp he leaped back, raising his hand to protect his face; the bent steel shaft sliced downwards, catching him hard on the forearm. He tried to jump clear, but his cloak was caught, snagged where it fastened around his throat, and as Mrs Mullarkey tried to raise her weapon to strike again he was jerked back towards her. She tugged at the jack handle, trying to free it, and rattled his jaw; he howled in pain. The warrior nearest tried to come to his aid, but Mrs Mullarkey was enclosed in the barrier and could not be reached. Only the steel handle protruded through the magical field; the warrior yelped and leaped back as it caught his hand a glancing blow.

'Nora Maura Margaret Mullarkey!' Conn yelled in fury, his head bouncing from side to side as Mrs Mullarkey tugged at her makeshift weapon. 'Stop! I *command* you!'

Mrs Mullarkey tugged again, yanking hard on the cloak and catching him on the throat. 'And I command you to shut your mouth, Fido!' she snarled furiously. 'You'll not use my name against me again!' she went on, striking angrily with almost every word. 'Because I went to the priest! And I had myself rechristened! *With an extra middle name!*'

She rained blows down upon the boy, jerking him back and forth by the collar like a rag doll.

Relief flooded Bansi. She felt a gentle hand on her shoulder and turned, glad to see her own relief echoed on her granny's face. 'I didn't think you could be rechristened,' she said quietly. 'And anyway, our teacher said it's a joining ceremony, not a naming ceremony.'

Granny chuckled dryly. 'Maybe; but if I were old Father Miley, and Nora Mullarkey banged on my door before sunrise, I dare say I'd do anything she wanted just to get the mad old haddock out of the house.'

'And if she believes that's given her a new name, then it has,' Pogo said. 'It's a funny thing, belief. Anyhow,' he added, 'I doubt he'll mess with her again! Here – what's that?'

For something odd was happening to the barrier. The waves of light that flowed around the jack handle as Mrs Mullarkey pounded at Conn were somehow peeling back, like flames burning a hole in a sheet of paper.

'The barrier's weakening,' the brownie muttered. 'I'm not sure that's a good thing.'

The cloak parted suddenly at the collar. Trailing a comet's tail of magical fire, it was hurled through the barrier, arcing high, to hit the rocky floor of the Hollow and flop in a crumpled heap almost at Bansi's feet. Mrs Mullarkey made one last lunge at Conn as the wolf-boy staggered out of her reach. 'And let that be a lesson to you, Fido!' she snapped, brandishing her weapon once more. Then she turned on her heels and marched triumphantly back to the others.

But where the jack handle had wrenched at the fabric of the barrier, a circle of flickering blue flames now hung, suspended, like a burning hole in the air. Bansi gazed at it, intrigued.

'Well, Nora,' Granny observed, 'that Dark Lord

chappy isn't going to be very pleased with you! Aside from hitting his doggy good and proper, it looks like you've broken his invisible wall, too!'

The Lord of the Dark Sidhe, however, looked far from displeased. Bansi watched him testing the area around the circle with his knife. The air rippled under the point, pushing back, refusing to be penetrated. Then, taking great care not to touch the flames, the Dark Lord pushed the blade into the very centre of the circle.

There was no resistance.

He smiled – an unpleasant, calculating smile that made Bansi's flesh creep – and regarded her thoughtfully. She stared back at him, determined not to be intimidated.

It was Pogo who realized what he was doing. 'Bansi! Look out!' he yelled – a moment too late.

Quick as thought, the Dark Lord's hand had already flashed up and back, its bone-white missile perfectly aimed straight through the gap towards Bansi's heart.

There was a sudden frantic fluttering. The Dark Lord whirled as the blade left his hand; something small and fast had exploded from a tunnel mouth above him. It plummeted, missing his face by inches, and shot like a dart through the flame-edged opening.

It was a bird – a swift, blue-grey blur of feather and beak and claw. As it passed through the torn barrier its wingtips brushed the unearthly fire. Blue flames caught it; leaped, licking hungrily, from feather to feather. It screeched in distress as it fell, flapping piteously and desperately, to the ground at Bansi's feet. In the talons of one foot, it clutched the white bone dagger.

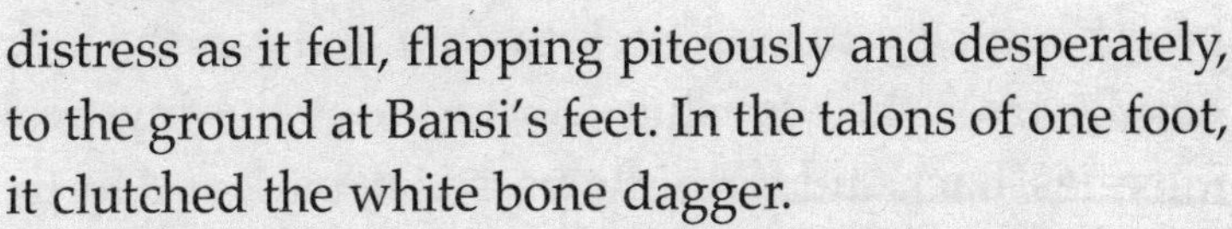

Then the falcon was stretching and shifting and changing, until Tam lay quivering in agony on the ground, the magical fire dancing in eerie triumph over his body. Bansi threw the wolfskin across him, ignoring Conn's roar of impotent fury, and knelt, pressing it down to smother the flames. Sparks leaped and crackled through the fur, discharging into the air around her. Ignoring them, she beat at the hide, determined to starve the fire and save her friend.

The flames rose through the pelt and wrapped themselves round her hands. She screamed as every nerve caught fire, an instant agony of scalding, scorching, poisonous pain. The unbearable burning spread up her forearms, inside and out; she could feel the flesh withering in the heat under her skin, the blood starting to boil and bubble.

She screamed again, fighting down the panic and the pain. Then Pogo was there, snatching the jack handle from Mrs Mullarkey and pressing it into her hands.

The steel shaft sucked the flames up greedily, and with them went the agony. In moments, she was whole again. She gasped with relief; caught her breath; quickly turned back to Tam and ran the jack handle over the wolfskin to draw out the mystical energies. Back and forth she passed it, back and forth, keeping the metal from actually touching the boy as it soaked up the magical fire. As swiftly as she could she bled the enchantment from his skin, leeching it away until none remained. Then she cast back the fur.

Tam stared up at her; blinked; shook his head.

'Ow!' he complained. 'That stung!' He winked and smiled a little unsteadily.

'Well,' Mrs Mullarkey said, 'and who might this be?'

'We've met, missus,' Tam said cheerily, stretching his limbs and checking that he truly was, after all, unharmed. 'Only you were having a wee nap, as I recall. Lying down on the floor in Bansi's room while the rest of us got on with things. It's good to see you with your eyes open.'

'This is Tam,' Granny explained, 'the púca I was telling you about.'

'Really?' Mrs Mullarkey said suspiciously. 'Not very goaty for a púca, is he?'

'Och, Nora, for goodness sake,' Granny said condescendingly, as she held up the wolfskin and began to check it for damage. 'All that goaty stuff is just something they do for fun. Don't you know anything about faeries?'

As Tam got to his feet, his customary grin back in place, Bansi felt her heart lift. That he could smile and joke after his ordeal, that he could recover so quickly, fuelled her hope and her confidence that he could help them. She smiled back and nodded down at the white knife at his feet.

'Thanks,' she said.

Tam picked the knife up. 'Ah, no problem,' he said, examining the blade and tucking it away. 'Well, not much. Apart from the agony and the near-death experience, that is.' He shook himself, as if testing his body out. 'But there's no after-effects – that's the main thing. Nice hearthrug,' he added, as Bansi's grandmother shook out the pelt and began to fold it.

'Isn't it, though?' said Granny, stroking it. 'Maybe we should get it made into a lovely warm coat.' She winked cheerily at Conn, who now stood staring in helpless rage through the barrier, hand to his injured throat.

'What's he up to now?' Pogo muttered.

Bansi turned her head. The Lord of the Dark Sidhe was pressing one hand gently against the barrier, near to the hole. The flames were leaping wildly as if Tam's passing had fed them and made them hungry for more. He muttered something, moved his hand, pressed again; muttered, pressed, moved. The air rippled with faint colours under his fingers.

'Well,' Tam ventured, 'at a guess, I'd say that bent iron bar, there–'

'*Steel* bar,' Granny put in, with a sideways glance at her friend.

'I'd say it weakened the barrier with all that waving around inside it, and now he's working out how to weaken it further. You know how it's easier to tear a piece of cloth once it's got a hole in it? He's trying to find out how to break the barrier enough to get in here at us.'

'Do you think he can?' Bansi asked, gripping the jack handle determinedly.

'Course he can,' muttered Pogo sourly. 'He's cunning as a fox, that one. He'll have some kind of counter-enchantment all set up and ready to go.'

'Aye,' Tam agreed. 'Only now, with the barrier

weakened, it'll take minutes instead of days. Then he'll be in here, and it'll all be over. And the sun's still going down out there; he'll get in while the light's still dying, all right. Unless we can fulfil the prophecy first.'

Bansi's eyes widened; in the midst of all their danger, she'd completely forgotten about the prophecy. 'Of course!' she said. 'That's why you brought me here in the first place! If we can just . . .' Her voice tailed off in confusion, as everything Pogo had told her about the Blood of the Morning Stars crowded into her memory. 'But you said all you had to do was bring me to one of your sacred places!'

'That's right, young man!' Granny agreed. 'Bansi's here, isn't she? Surely that's the prophecy fulfilled!'

Tam shook his head. 'That's what we thought. But if the power was returning to Tir na n'Óg, wouldn't we know about it by now? And who was it brought you to Balor's Hollow?'

'The wolf-boy,' said Bansi. 'Conn.'

'Aye, well,' Tam said. 'Take a look at him. Does he look like he's just come into the inheritance of Derga?' Bansi glanced over to where Conn stood, glaring in impotent, sullen fury and still clutching his wounded throat. 'No, if the prophecy had been fulfilled, we'd know about it. There's something we're missing.'

Bansi thought furiously. 'Pogo,' she said, 'how did the prophecy start? What were the exact words?'

Pogo's brow wrinkled. '*When the Blood of the Morning Stars, joined and flowing together, is returned at last to the sacred earth as the light dies, then–*'

'Hang on,' Bansi broke in. 'It doesn't say "sacred place", it says "sacred earth" . . .'

'Same thing.' Pogo frowned. 'The only sacred earth I know of is in the sacred places . . .'

'No, but maybe it's *not* the same thing,' Bansi insisted. 'Look at the ground. This isn't earth, it's rock.'

Pogo shook his little head gloomily. 'The rock is of the earth, and on the earth, and in the earth. I can't see it makes a difference.'

'Aye, but wait, that could be it!' Tam broke in animatedly. 'There's a big crack in the rock over there; you should be able to get your feet into it. It's worth a try.' A determined look came over his face, an expression at odds with the carefree smiling face that Bansi felt she had come to know so well. '*Anything's* worth a try,' he added, his tone strange and grim.

Bansi ran to the crack and squeezed one foot in behind the other. She turned hopefully to Tam and Pogo. 'Anything happening?'

They looked at each other, paused, shook their heads.

'Your shoes!' Granny said. 'Maybe it should be your skin touching the earth!'

It made sense. Bansi crouched down, pushed her hand into the crack, pressed against the ground. The soil felt ancient and dry and dusty and dead.

'Now?' she asked.

Tam moved to her and knelt down with her. His fingers scratched at the soil, as if hoping they could help her awaken it. 'Nothing,' he said. 'There's nothing. The power of Tir na n'Óg still sleeps.'

'So the prophecy was wrong?' Bansi asked, standing. The others gathered round her anxiously.

Tam shook his head again. His perpetual air of merriment seemed to have completely deserted him. 'It can't be wrong. *We* were wrong. It's the only explanation. We were mistaken.' He clasped her arm gently. 'The prophecy didn't mean what we thought it did. But we still have to fulfil it. And there's only one way I can think of.'

Bansi screwed up her face in puzzlement. 'How, though? What *does* it mean, if . . . ?' Then she realized. 'Tam, no!'

He flashed her a handsome, rueful grin. 'Sorry, Bansi, it's nothing personal. I'll make it quick.'

One lightning-fast foot struck, stamped, hard and sudden, knocking Pogo off-balance and pinning him down in one deft move. A hand lashed out, flinging dry soil in the old women's faces, blinding them, leaving them wiping frantically at their streaming eyes. The other hand tightened its grip, twisted Bansi round, pulled her in towards him: in a single movement, he had her.

An instant later, the white bone knife was at her throat.

Chapter Twenty-Four

Bansi pushed furiously against Tam's grip. She felt the blade resting lightly on her skin; strained with both hands to keep it from cutting her. In front of her she could see Granny and Mrs Mullarkey, still blinded, stumbling hopelessly across the circle.

'They can't help you,' Tam said. 'I put a wee enchantment on that fistful of soil – nothing beside what the Dark Lord can do, but it'll keep them out of the way until . . . well, until it's too late.'

'Tam, wait!' Bansi spoke as calmly as she could, though she felt sure he must be able to hear her heart pounding frantically. She held herself still, bracing her arms against his knife-hand, afraid that the slightest movement would send the blade slicing through her throat. 'Please! You don't have to do this!'

She felt him shrug. 'Afraid I do. Sorry. No hard feelings, eh?'

'No hard feelings?' Pogo growled from underfoot, vainly struggling to free himself. 'You've got a knife to her throat! Just let me up, Tam, and I'll show you hard feelings, all right!'

'But *why*, Tam?' The unfairness of it suddenly hit Bansi like a blow to the stomach: for smiling, carefree Tam to turn on her like this when she thought he'd come to help her. She felt her eyes prickle as unwanted tears rose; furiously, she blinked them away. 'I thought you were my friend!' she said, hating herself for how weak it sounded.

'Friend?' Pogo spat venomously. 'He's a púca. Púcas don't have friends. They don't know how. How long have you been plotting this, Tam?'

'Ah, be fair, now, both of you,' Tam said. 'I'm just doing what has to be done for the good of Tir na n'Óg. And I would do anything – *anything* – to stop it from falling into the Dark Lord's hands. If Derga's inheritance becomes his, he'll seize the realm of Faery like a ripe plum and swallow it whole.' He nodded towards where the Lord of the Dark Sidhe now stood, face cold with rage, eyes focused on the hole in the barrier, hands held out as if drawing power from the air. 'See? He's nearly ready now. In a minute he'll be through, and there'll be nothing we can do to stop him killing Bansi. She's dead anyway, Pogo. The only question is who kills her.' He sighed. 'I'm sorry about this, Bansi, I really am. You got any last requests?'

Bansi's pride burned at the thought of asking her captor for anything; but she had to. 'If you mean that, Tam,' she said, her voice trembling, 'then find my mum and dad. Promise me you'll rescue them.'

Tam cleared his throat. 'Your parents? Ah. Well. You don't need to worry about them. The fact of the matter is, they never were in any danger. They were never kidnapped. They're still back at your granny's house.'

'*What?*' Pogo exploded. 'Why, you—'

'What you saw – the room overturned, your parents gone – it was a glamour. An illusion. I made it look like they'd been taken, but they were there all the time, sleeping peacefully. Probably still are. I cast a wee enchantment over them, so they wouldn't get woken in all the fuss.'

A cold fist of betrayal twisted in Bansi's gut. 'You mean – you tricked me into coming here? You've been planning this all along?' She breathed in, a long, deep breath, as if trying to suck back all the bad feelings that were rising up inside her. 'You brought me here to kill me?'

'I should never have trusted you, Tam!' Pogo spat, still vainly struggling against the púca's weight. 'Is this what you meant when you said to Caithne, "No matter if the girl dies"? That you were planning to kill her yourself?'

'No! I never planned this! I honestly thought all we had to do was to bring you to one of the sacred places. That's what I've always believed the prophecy meant, and that's all I planned to do, Bansi – persuade you to come to Tir na n'Óg; take you to one of the sacred places; get you home again. That's all I was going to do. But, yes, I tricked you. I had to. The risk was too great otherwise . . .'

'Risk?' Pogo stormed, arms and legs thrashing angrily in a futile attempt to break free from the foot that pinned him down. '*Risk?* You swore an oath, Tam! You swore an oath to Caithne and the whole company, to the fellowship of the Sacred Grove, that you'd guard the girl in the mortal world, and keep her safe–'

'No, Pogo. I swore to the company I'd abide by their decision. And I've done that.'

'You've *what*?' Pogo spluttered. 'Are you mad? We agreed that we should keep the Blood of the Morning Stars away from Tir na n'Óg–'

'No, Pogo,' Tam interrupted, and Bansi, fighting her own fear and sadness, almost wondered if she could hear regret in his voice. 'We needed you if we were to find Bansi before the Dark Sidhe did, but you made it clear you'd never go along with any decision to bring her here. So the company pretended to agree to do it your way; but secretly we decided I should bring Bansi to Tir na n'Óg – whatever it took.'

All the fight seemed suddenly to leave Pogo's body. He lay as if crushed under Tam's boot, head and limbs flopping weakly on the ground. 'What – you mean that Caithne . . . ?'

The knife at Bansi's throat moved slightly as Tam nodded. 'Caithne, Aed Firetongue, Bindweed – all of us. Everyone except you, Pogo – and Flooter; we couldn't have trusted him to keep it quiet. But the rest of us were all in agreement. It was too risky to do what you wanted – to guard Bansi until the gate closed. What if we'd failed? What if the Dark Sidhe had got her? So I cast a glamour over her parents' room; pretended they'd been kidnapped; persuaded her to come to Tir na n'Óg with us. And persuaded you to go along with it. I never thought it would end up like this, though. And I'm truly sorry it has. Truly I am. There's no time left, now. I'm sorry, Bansi. Hold still and it won't hurt a bit, I promise.'

Slowly, he began to force the dagger closer. Bansi felt her arms begin to give way; she pushed harder, but to no avail.

'Tam, please! Think about what you're doing! This'll make you as bad as the Dark Lord! And you can't be! You can't!'

'Maybe I am, though. He'll kill you to gain power over Tir na n'Óg; I'll kill you to stop him. It could be there's no difference between us at all. I'd have let you live if there was any other way, mind you, and I truly wish there was. But I will *never* bow to the Lord of the Dark Sidhe – or any other tyrant – if I can help it; and if killing you's the only way out of it, then that's what I'll do. And I have to do it now. For the sake of Tir na—'

And then he yelled and dropped the knife. The pressure against Bansi's hands gave way, and without thinking she pushed, squirmed, forced herself free of his grip, stumbling on the rocky ground as she turned.

Flooter was swinging by the teeth from Tam's wrist, his jaws clamped tight. Tam flailed and thrashed his arm through the air in a vain attempt to shake him off, but Flooter hardly seemed to notice. He tried to tap the side of his nose knowingly; missed wildly as Tam whirled him round.

'Nrrrgrrdy knrrrws hrrw thrr clrrrrcrrng trrvrrv!' he mumbled cheerfully, and his grip slackened.

He let go, landed with a thump. 'Not even the cluricaun!' he added, sitting up. 'Here, Pogo! I've kept her safe again! How'sh about that key?'

But Pogo was too busy to answer. Freed from under Tam's foot, he rushed for the jack handle, grabbed it, swung it violently. Tam dodged nimbly, caught the little man with a kick in the back that sent him and his weapon flying in opposite directions. Swivelling, he leaped through the air, shouldered Bansi aside as she reached for the fallen knife, seized it, flew at her, white blade slashing out wildly as he grabbed for her. In mere moments he had her again: one wiry arm round her waist, the other fighting to bring the bone knife to her neck. Hot pain sliced across her thumb as she threw both her hands on to his and struggled to hold the dagger away. A raw, stark shout of fury and desperation burst from her; she felt his strength overpowering hers, saw the evil gleam of the white blade drawing ever nearer to her unprotected throat . . .

And then Tam howled in pain and dropped the knife as Pogo, with a mighty leap, brought the jack handle down hard upon his wrist. A twist of steel as the brownie landed, and Tam's feet were knocked out from under him. A bound, and Pogo was on his former friend's chest, one end of the crooked metal shaft pressed firmly and painfully into the púca's throat.

'Not a move, Tam,' he warned.

Tam grimaced. 'You fool, Pogo,' he said hoarsely. 'She'll die in any case.'

'Then I'll die protecting her.'

'So you'll both be dead. What good will that do? And what's the life of one mortal child against the whole of Tir na n'Óg? It's not me who's the traitor, Pogo. You've betrayed us all.'

Bansi stooped and picked up the white bone knife. The hilt felt somehow greasy and uneasy in her hand. Her skin crawled as she held it, and her fingers revolted at its touch; she had to force them not to drop it as she held it out.

'Pogo,' she said, 'can you use this creepy thing instead? If you can stand to hold it, that is. I need the steel to help Granny and Mrs Mullarkey.'

Pogo, not taking his eyes from Tam, held out his free hand and took the knife. 'That's the feel of dark magic, that is,' he told her, pressing the blade against Tam's throat and passing her the jack handle. 'I wouldn't want to hold it for long – but then I don't think we've *got* long.'

Even as he spoke, an eerie noise swelled: a droning, throbbing, unmusical chant that issued from the throats of the courtiers of the Dark Sidhe on their high balcony. Bansi shuddered; the feeling the sound gave her was the same revulsion she'd felt as she held the knife. Moments later, the drums started up again – a slow, doom-laden pounding, quite different from the wild drumming of before but no less sinister.

Granny and Mrs Mullarkey were both sitting helplessly on the ground nearby, eyes streaming. It was a matter of moments to break Tam's enchantment with the touch of steel.

'This is a fine time for a sing-song,' Granny muttered grimly, blinking up at the gallery. 'Not much of a song, mind you. It would help if it had a tune, for instance.'

'What are they doing?' Bansi asked Pogo.

It was Tam, though, who answered, his voice rough and weak. 'They're adding their magic to the Dark Lord's. That's what they were doing before, with all the dancing – soaking the atmosphere with enchantment. Even he could never have created the barrier otherwise. And now, they're helping him destroy it again. Or at least part of it – enough to get through.'

'When he does, I wonder if he'd be happy to kill you instead of Bansi,' said Mrs Mullarkey, rising to her feet. 'I'll give him a hand.'

And then the chanting grew louder, and as it did, Bansi saw for a moment a flickering in the air between the two stones on either side of the fiery hole. The sidhe warriors, smiling hungrily, gathered around the Dark Lord; the courtiers stared down malevolently as they chanted. Every eye was fixed on Bansi. The Lord of the Dark Sidhe, bathed in a strange light that seemed to come from within, pierced her with his poisonous yellow gaze; his hands reached out as if to tear the barrier in two. Conn, smiling coldly and wickedly, stood at his side, his injuries forgotten. The stance of his body spoke of his eagerness to kill.

Between the two standing stones in front of the Dark Lord, the barrier began to shimmer. The flames around the burning circle flared. Iridescent light bloomed, the colours rising stronger and brighter as the chanting grew louder and the air thrummed with its weird harmonies. The hot, intense scents of incense and bitter cinnamon filled Bansi's head, drowning out everything except a profound nausea and a loud, violent roaring that seemed to go on for ever. The jack handle grew warm in her hands; she breathed deeply and, with an effort, stood tall and straight, defying her enemies.

Beside her, Granny and Mrs Mullarkey crumpled to the ground, hands pressed uselessly to their ears. Pogo collapsed, writhing, and rolled off Tam's chest; Tam curled into a ball and lay shuddering feverishly.

Flooter had vanished again, as mysteriously as he had appeared.

Gripping her steely weapon, Bansi stood alone.

All around them, coruscating brightness sparked and flashed from stone to stone and back again. Bright blue bolts of mystical energy leaped the gap.

The unearthly chanting grew like a surging wave, swelling into a single painful chord that held and held, throbbing and echoing painfully inside her head.

The roaring grew louder.

Like a curtain tearing, the portion of the barrier between the two stones on either side of the burning, suspended circle began to peel from top to bottom, opening a doorway for their enemies to reach them.

Chapter Twenty-Five

In front of the Lord of the Dark Sidhe the magical barrier sparked and faded, sparked and faded. Flames guttered between the two stones. His warriors watched impatiently, eager to push at last into the circle; only seconds remained before the way was clear.

Bansi's head spun nightmarishly. The walls and stones of Balor's Hollow blurred and distorted before her eyes. A relentless, surging feeling of sickness swept over her again and again, each wave deeper than the last, and her skull vibrated painfully with the low, rumbling roar of the dark magic.

She clenched the jack handle and felt it grow warm, warmer still. The nausea began to fade; her vision began to clear; the strength began to flood back into her limbs. She gripped the steel shaft more tightly; it throbbed and pulsed as it absorbed the enchantment that swam around her.

Now it was glowing; and like a wave of clear bright water breaking over her, she was released from the spell. She stood, renewed, and breathed deeply, clasping the jack handle in both hands.

The singers on the balcony gave a single victorious shout as the last surge of magical energies sputtered between the two stones, and then all was silence save the roaring sound, now diminished to a distant undertone.

The Lord of the Dark Sidhe strode through the gap into the circle, eager to deliver the killing blow. His entourage followed respectfully, stopping at a distance.

Bansi hefted the jack handle and faced her enemy.

The Dark Lord smiled humourlessly. 'Not exactly a warrior's weapon, is it?' he remarked. 'Conn!' Without taking his eyes off Bansi, he held his hand out. 'Arm me, if you please.'

Conn snatched a sword from the nearest warrior and threw it high; it spun for his master in a mesmerizing arc. Without turning, without even glancing at it, the Dark Lord snatched it from the air, turning it expertly in his hand. The gleaming bronze blade danced threateningly in front of Bansi's face.

Bansi stepped back, the clumsy, unbalanced weight of her own weapon heavy and uncooperative in her hand. The distant roar grew slowly, menacingly louder.

'With less ceremony than I'd have liked, perhaps,'

the Lord of the Dark Sidhe remarked, 'but your blood will be spilt.'

Mockingly he bowed and raised his sword. Suddenly the bright blade flashed out. Bansi parried clumsily; the sword twisted, catching the jack handle easily, tearing it from her hands. Immediately the heavy enchantment pressed down on her, drugging her senses, weighing her down.

The Lord of the Dark Sidhe smiled cruelly. The sword flicked up, its point grazing Bansi's throat. She tried to step back and found herself held as if from behind. The roaring swelled, filling her head; an oddly familiar sound, more mechanical than magical, out of place in some way.

'This,' the Dark Lord said coolly, 'is a moment to savour. The moment of my victory. The moment when I return the Blood of the Morning Stars to the sacred earth of Tir na n'Óg.' The vicious blade coldly caressed Bansi's throat. 'The question is, child, how long can I make that moment last? You have defied me most audaciously, after all. But in vain; for I have won; and now the inheritance of Derga will be mine!' He raised his voice as the roaring rose towards a triumphant crescendo. It filled Balor's Hollow, echoing loudly from the cliff-like walls, growing like a living thing.

The Dark Lord's eyes flicked sideways, a

fragment of doubt entering them for the first time. He looked up at his courtiers.

'Who,' he demanded loudly, 'is responsible for that noise?'

The courtiers of the Dark Sidhe, high on their stone balcony, looked at each other in puzzlement. They shrugged; one or two called something to their master, but the roaring was now so loud that nothing else could be heard.

And then, gleaming like an armoured monster, its headlights blazing like the eyes of an awakened dragon, the dark green Morris Minor Traveller burst from the tunnel mouth behind them. The courtiers panicked; were scattered; most leaped or were pushed off the gallery. The huge drums toppled and smashed on the rocky floor below.

The car accelerated, soaring high over Bansi's head to land with a bounce in the centre of the circle, and executed a perfect handbrake turn to aim itself directly at the Lord of the Dark Sidhe.

Behind its wheel, no driver could be seen.

The Dark Lord, astonished, leaped aside. The car twisted in hungry pursuit. Its gleaming mouth-like grille bore down on him again, scattering his warriors as they tried to defend him. He threw himself into the air, somersaulting over the car with incredible agility. Even as he leaped, its wheels locked; it skidded round once more, its front wing catching him a glancing blow as he landed. He flinched as he tumbled against the nearest standing stone; leaped high as the car turned on him yet again.

Perhaps it was because the Dark Lord's hold on her was weakened by the distraction that Bansi suddenly discovered she could move. Without wasting a second she grabbed the steel jack handle and felt the drowsiness of enchantment fall away.

Her companions were beginning to stir, the agonies that had pinned them down slowly receding at last. Quickly she moved among them, using the touch of steel once more to free first her granny, then Mrs Mullarkey and Pogo. Finally, reluctantly, she laid the jack handle across Tam's chest, not at all moved by the cries of distress he let out as she did so.

Mrs Mullarkey stood with her mouth agape. 'Well,' she exclaimed, as the machine turned on the Dark Lord once more, harrying him away from them, 'I always said that car had a mind of its own.'

'Mind of its own, nothing!' spluttered Granny. 'It's possessed by a demon, that's what it is! Which,' she added, absently picking up Conn's wolfskin and folding it like a freshly laundered cardigan, 'explains an awful lot about the way you drive, Nora.'

Bansi stepped forward and swung as Conn, spying his precious cloak in Granny's hands, leaped as if from nowhere. The jack handle connected with a satisfying thud, knocking the wolf-boy halfway across the circle, where he slammed into an unbroken portion of the barrier and lay momentarily stunned.

The car turned again, screeching loudly in a way that made Mrs Mullarkey wince, and aimed for a line of courtiers who were shakily picking themselves up off the cracked stone floor after their long steel-induced fall from the balcony. They turned and ran, fleeing for their lives, and like some great mechanical predator the car swerved after them.

'The barrier!' someone cried, and several courtiers hastily fled back through the newly-made opening to the safety of its magical protection.

The car made straight for them.

With a great swirling and sparking of magical energy across its steel bonnet, it plunged through the enchanted boundary, scattering the courtiers in utter panic. The weakened barrier flared and ignited, bursting into flames which spread around the circle and, as suddenly, were gone.

The car lurched across the circle and came to a sudden stop inches from a standing stone. Gears ground as someone tried to find reverse; and then the rear doors of the Traveller burst open. A tide of brownies poured out, armed to the teeth from Granny's boxes of scrap iron.

The Dark Sidhe stopped and stared. One or two laughed disbelievingly; then another, and another. The laughter grew louder and more unpleasant as they gathered together around their master. The Dark Lord stepped forward, his expression a blend of anger and scorn.

'You?' he scoffed. 'The smallest, weakest tribe in the whole realm of Tir na n'Óg, and you dare challenge *me*? On your knees, little ones! Beg my forgiveness, swear yourselves to my service, and perhaps I may let you live!' Stepping forward, he lashed out with his foot, aiming a vicious kick at the nearest brownie.

He yelled in pain as an iron candlestick, swung with equal and opposite force, connected smartly with his shin.

Outraged at this offence, the Dark Sidhe drew their swords. They spread out, surrounding the tiny brownies like cats circling mice, their arrogant postures betraying an unspoken assumption of strength, power and the right to rule.

The Dark Lord muttered an angry incantation and thrust out his hand. A sudden wind whipped around him, ruffling his hair, filling out his cloak. Without warning, it rose up and blasted itself hard at the brownie tribe. It was a simple magic, but it should have been enough to sweep the little people off their feet and toss them into the air, making them easy sport for the poised weapons of his courtiers.

The brownies raised their own weapons, their motley arsenal of iron odds and ends.

The magical wind simply died around them.

In an instant the brownies fell upon the Dark Sidhe, ducking under their swords and scurrying up their bodies, swarming all over them, swiping and hammering at them with unrelenting iron. At such close range, the blades of the Dark Sidhe were worse than useless, endangering one another far more than they did their tiny foes.

The Lord of the Dark Sidhe howled once more, this time with rage, and threw himself into the battle. He kicked and fought furiously, but for every brownie he knocked aside two more sprang forward, swinging their makeshift weapons. They clung to his legs, clambered up his cloak, pounded and beat at him with cold hard iron until he fell to his knees like a great lion brought down by hyenas. With a tremendous roar he forced himself to his feet once more, unclasped his cloak and let it fall, the brownies falling with it. Before they had a chance to renew the attack, he had vanished into the dark shadows of Balor's Hollow.

Seeing him flee, his followers lost all courage. With anguished cries of pain and despair they turned and took flight, each one pursued by a horde of exhilarated brownies. Their cries rang around the walls of Balor's Hollow; their footsteps clattered and faded along the tunnels.

And suddenly they were gone, and at last Bansi and her friends were safe.

With a sigh of relief, Bansi sat down on the hard, rocky ground. She looked at Pogo, who – for the first time since she'd met him – was very nearly smiling.

'How did that happen?' he asked in amazement. 'Brownies standing up for themselves? Wielding iron in anger? I was nearly thrown out of the tribe just for suggesting such a thing! What changed their minds?'

'Bansi did,' a voice said. The driver's door of the Morris Minor Traveller swung open and Moina hopped out, a huge grin on her tiny brown face. She rushed to Pogo and hugged him, laughing at his puzzlement. 'In part, at least.' She turned to Bansi. 'The tribe were curious because you had escaped the Brúid creature, even for a while,' she explained. 'So they followed in secret as I led you to the forest's edge; and we all watched as you faced it even though you had no hope of defeating it. But you won! Some argued that it was not an honourable victory; but others held that your courage was honour enough. I told them, too, what you had said about letting others make the laws that work against us, and after some discussion many agreed with you.'

'And then I pointed out how much fun it would be to belt the Dark Sidhe with lumps of iron, and that settled it,' cawed the raven, hopping out behind her. 'And before you go off complaining about how long it took us to get here, it's not my fault, OK? The brownies insisted on tidying the car first.'

It was true: the Traveller was a different car from the battered wreck they had left at the edge of the forest. The dents had been hammered out, the puncture repaired, the inside swept clean; only the occasional scratch and the empty frame where the broken window had been gave any hint of what the car had been through.

'And then, of course,' Moina added, 'we had to work out how to make it move. Not easy when you need three people to steer and another for each of the pedals.'

'Not to menshun the hand brake!' slurred yet another familiar voice; and Flooter toppled out of the car, landing flat on his face. He picked himself up and grinned blurrily at Pogo. 'Now,' he said shiftily, 'about that key . . .'

Bansi smiled, and shook her head. Then her gaze fell upon Tam, and her smile died.

He was sitting against one of the standing stones, clearly in pain. The magical assaults had taken their toll on him, and the touch of steel had been almost as bad as the enchantment it had lifted.

'It's not over yet,' he murmured.

'It is for you,' Pogo told him sharply. 'You'll not get the chance to betray Bansi again, that's for sure.'

Tam shook his head. 'You really won't see it, will you, Pogo? The Dark Sidhe will find her yet. Or if not the Dark Sidhe, someone else – the Unseelie Court, maybe, or some solitary Hag. One of them will find her, and she'll die, and we'll all be enslaved.' He coughed, and wiped his mouth. 'My money's still on the Dark Sidhe.'

'Very wise,' said a voice. Every head snapped round in horror; for although none of them could tell where it had come from, it was a voice they all recognized. The voice of the Lord of the Dark Sidhe.

And then one of the standing stones reached out, grabbed Bansi O'Hara's grandmother and swallowed her whole.

There was a frozen moment of horror during which the assembled company tried to make sense of what they had seen. Then, without any of them understanding how, and without anything changing, it became clear that this particular stone was not a stone; had never been a stone. All this time, the Lord of the Dark Sidhe and his faithful wolf-boy Conn had been standing among them, hidden by a magic that deceived the eye, that told lies about the shape of things.

Now Conn stood cruelly gripping Eileen O'Hara. One of his arms pinned both of hers to her body; the other hand was twisted into her grey hair, forcing her head back to expose her throat. His mouth was open in a savage smile; the threat was clear.

'Stay very still,' the Dark Lord said, 'and the old woman may live. For now. Defy me, and she will certainly die.' He stepped forward and inclined his head in an ironic bow. 'By rights, child, I should kill you slowly. Very slowly. But I grow weary of this, and eager to claim my destiny. So here is what I propose: surrender, and your death will be quick. As soon as the sacrifice is made, your companions will be free to go. Resist me, or try to flee, and Conn will hunt you down, and bring you to me; and you will die screaming for mercy. But not before the old woman meets a sudden and painful end. Which she will do in any case, within the minute, if you do not come to me now.'

Put like that, it seemed there was no decision to be made.

As Bansi began the slow walk to her death, everything came into focus in a new way, as if her mind was determined to savour her last few moments of life. It was strange how it almost felt as if she was someone else, watching and hearing and sensing from a hidden place inside her. Everything impressed itself at once on her consciousness; the dusty smell of the air, the beating of her heart.

And the throbbing in her left thumb. Surprised, she stopped and looked down at the thin, straight wound, remembering the hot pain as she'd wrestled with Tam's knife-hand. The thick redness of her blood welled from the shallow cut.

The Lord of the Dark Sidhe strode casually towards her, knife ready for the sacrifice. Pogo's words echoed in her head:

'When the Blood of the Morning Stars, joined and flowing together at last, is returned to the sacred earth as the light dies, then shall the power of Tir na n'Óg awaken. Then shall the ways between the worlds reopen. And the one who returns the blood to the land shall come into the inheritance of Derga.'

And suddenly, with tremendous clarity, it came to her that there was one chance left.

Chapter Twenty-Six

'*When the Blood of the Morning Stars, joined and flowing together, is returned at last to the sacred earth . . .*'

Bansi dropped to the ground. Her bleeding thumb throbbed hotly as she thrust it into a wide crack in the stone and pressed it hard against the dry soil.

Then the Dark Lord was upon her, grabbing a fistful of hair and yanking her head back hard, exposing her throat to the pitiless blade of the white knife.

And . . .

. . . time . . .

. . . stopped.

Or perhaps it was that Bansi's mind accelerated. Her limbs, even her eyes, suddenly felt as if they were trapped in thick jelly – not heavy, not paralysed, but working against such huge resistance that the slightest movement could take for ever. The Dark Lord, too, and all those around them – Conn, Granny, Mrs Mullarkey, Pogo, Tam, Moina, Flooter, the raven

– appeared to have frozen in time. Even the flaming torch she could see ahead of her had paused in mid-flicker, its flame caught and held in petrified motion.

The pulse in her wounded thumb came again; but immensely, intensely slowly and with an incredible heat which seemed to flow from her body and down, down into the earth. Suddenly it was as if her whole self was surging out through the narrow cut, forcing itself out of her body, joining with the world beneath her. She felt dizzy, light-headed, and yet somehow strangely aware; although she had no words for it she could almost have sworn that she was touching an existence she had never dreamed of.

The flow reversed. Sensation and consciousness flooded her, awakening and refreshing her like a cool stream on a hot day, as if her mind, her very being, was filling up with knowledge and wisdom and perception beyond measure or understanding. For an instant, it was as if the whole world was hers to command; as if she could see and hear and touch and understand all of it, every last blade of grass and grain of sand, the smallest insect, the vastest ocean and all the life and light and darkness therein.

As that instant faded and her mind returned to her, she realized all this had taken place within a single breath. She felt her lungs slowly, slowly begin to exhale; and as they did, a glow appeared in front of her – a pinprick of light at first, right before her eyes, which grew and blossomed and expanded into a dazzling white glare that filled the whole of Balor's Hollow. It should, she felt later, have been so bright as to be painful; and yet somehow it caused her no hurt at all. And within it were two forms: a woman and a man, tall and beautiful and regal; and Bansi knew that these were her ancestors Caer and Avalloc, the Morning Stars of Tir na n'Óg. They turned to her, smiled warmly, and began to fade.

Just before they disappeared, Bansi saw Caer's lips move and heard just two words.

'Be quick.'

And then the light died.

Her chest suddenly contracted, expanded, contracted. It took her a moment to recognize that she was breathing again. Her thumb throbbed with a regular pulse; she could feel her heart beating. She blinked. Across the circle the flame of the torch was still held motionless, like an oil painting, but in an instant her body had quickened.

She raised her arm – how easy that suddenly felt! – and shoved the Dark Lord's knife-hand out of the way; then she reached up, untwisted her hair from his grip, and stood. It was a strange feeling, being free to move around the circle when, for the others, time had stopped, leaving them as motionless as the great standing stones.

No . . . not quite as motionless. As she looked at Conn, it seemed that something was subtly different about the wolf-boy. She looked closer, more carefully. His eyes were wider, as if in disbelief – and so were his jaws. With imperceptible slowness, he was edging closer to her grandmother's throat, ready to tear it out.

Angrily, Bansi wrenched her granny free from his grip and pushed him, hard, knocking him to the ground. It was surprisingly easy. As an afterthought she scooped a handful of dry earth from the cracked ground, packed it into his mouth, and clapped his jaw shut. Then she looked round at the Lord of the Dark Sidhe. His knife-hand was flung further back now, she was sure, and the weapon itself was beginning to slip from his grasp. As she watched, it began to move visibly, his fingers releasing it in slow-motion until it hung suspended, slipping at a snail's pace through the air.

Then it was sliding more quickly – still unbelievably slowly, from Bansi's point of view, but its movement was detectable without staring; and the others in the circle were starting to move in the same sluggish slow-motion way.

Bansi plucked the dagger from the air, and

shuddered. In this accelerated state, the feeling of wrongness was multiplied to one of evil, as if the knife possessed a malevolent will of its own. Seized with the desire to get rid of it, she dashed its point against the nearest stone, hoping to blunt it at least, or shatter the blade if she could.

To her surprise, it sank into the stone as though into butter or honey – easily, and with no resistance – and stuck there, firm and immoveable. She tugged at it, but it would not come free.

Time around her was definitely moving faster, or else Bansi herself was dropping out of whatever strange acceleration had held her; for the friends and enemies around her were clearly moving now, slow and ponderous as great snails – all but the little cluricaun who, frozen in time like the others a moment before, had once again vanished.

To the Lord of the Dark Sidhe, things looked very different. He had been on the point of slitting Bansi's throat, about to spill her blood onto the sacred earth and claim the inheritance of Derga, when suddenly his fingers, gripping her hair, had been twisted agonizingly apart. Simultaneously a huge force had knocked the knife from his grasp, wrenching his shoulder painfully. His captive had disappeared; the dagger had vanished as it left his hand. Conn released his own prisoner and was suddenly on the ground, choking and retching. A blur of motion caught his eye; there was the knife, buried to the hilt in one of the stones. Beside it, a shimmering haze resolved itself into Bansi O'Hara, albeit slightly vague around the edges.

His dignity forsaken, the Lord of the Dark Sidhe ran at her, fury and alarm fighting for possession of his senses. Bansi blurred again, not quite vanishing as she moved aside at the last moment with astonishing speed. A shaft of pain shot through his injured shoulder as he careered into the stone. He let out a yell of pain and turned; she looked more solid now, more real, but as he reached out for her she stepped back quickly. Impossibly quickly.

Anger clouded his mind, dulled his thinking. Growling with rage, he turned on the girl's grandmother, thinking to use her as a hostage.

Another haze of motion, and Bansi collided with him, her momentum hitting him hard, hurling him gracelessly to the ground. But she was slowing; he could see her more distinctly by the minute. He sprang to his feet, turning as he did so, following her with his eyes, drawing strength and power from the enchantment-charged environment.

Behind him, Conn spat and retched and gasped. He rose to his knees and found himself staring once more at the steel jack handle.

'If you know what's good for you, Fido,' Mrs Mullarkey observed, 'you'll roll over and play dead like a good wee doggy.' Conn looked up into her face, and growled. 'I said, *down*, boy!' she commanded, jabbing at him painfully. He yelped and lay sullenly back on the ground.

Bansi slowed, dropping gradually back into normal time. The Lord of the Dark Sidhe pinned her with his gaze, tracking her as a hunter tracks his prey. The air crackled around him.

'Give up, child,' he said, his voice dripping enchantment. 'I have ensured that the very air of this place is saturated with magic; and so I am master here. You cannot win.'

His words thrummed and throbbed around her, pushing at the boundaries of her mind; and yet somehow her head remained clear.

'I think I've won already,' she said. 'Whether you kill me or not, you won't get what you want.' She held up her dusty, injured thumb.

The Dark Lord looked at her without comprehension and shook his head. 'No,' he said, and the wind began to whip around him once more. 'Now I will win. And you will die.'

The last syllable stretched out, changing as it did so into a long unearthly cry. It seemed to come from many voices, and from somewhere else, as though his throat had become the gateway into another world. Lights flickered around him, wraithlike lights which sucked the brightness from the torchlight and vomited out shadows that capered and cavorted in the air before him.

'He's mad!' whispered Tam.

'Aye, well, we knew that,' Granny said tersely.

'No, but . . . If he's doing what I think he's doing . . . he could kill us all!'

'Och, well, as if he hasn't been trying to do that all day! Which puts him in good company,' she added with pointed sarcasm.

Bansi circled the Dark Lord warily; he turned, keeping her in view. The howling noise issued from his lips and kept coming, sustained far beyond the capacity of any mortal breath. His yellow eyes gleamed and sparkled. The cavernous Hollow darkened around him as the uncanny lights wove a cocoon of radiance and shade, a pulsating shell of mystical energy at whose core he stood, consumed with rage and greed and malice. It flared brightly, flared again, reaching out, touching the faces of everyone present with raw, malignant power. They felt its brightness, its heat, its deadly force; and all of them shuddered.

All except one. In the midst of the storm, Bansi O'Hara felt a strange calmness within. It was as if she was guided by a loving voice – or two voices, speaking in perfect unity. She stood tall, looking up at the Lord of the Dark Sidhe and the lethal writhing that surrounded him, and she was not afraid.

She knew what to do.

As the dark force flashed out again, she stepped forward. It was like walking into a furnace; the supernatural, evil heat of the Dark Lord's magic threatened to consume her in an instant; and just for a moment, her resolve faltered. But the feeling came again, as if two well-loved voices – at once just like and yet somehow unlike her parents' – were encouraging her, *Go on, go on.*

She stepped forward again, and stared into those wicked yellow eyes, eyes that were filled with hatred and badness and the sheer malicious joy of destruction, and she saw them open wide and greedy and gleeful in anticipation of his final victory.

Bansi O'Hara relaxed in the scorching fire of his magical onslaught. She felt something change inside her, as if those two voices had found a switch and gently thrown it.

And she breathed in.

The fire entered her lungs; it filled up her chest; it pushed up into her head and out into her limbs. And still she breathed in. She did not stop; she could not stop. The swirling, coruscating energies around the

Dark Lord were drawn unremittingly into her until she felt as if she would burst; and still they filled her. She felt she would drown; the noise of dark magic hammered in her ears like the pulsing of panicked blood. And still she breathed in, as if her lungs were infinite, elastic, unending. She absorbed the magic that the Lord of the Dark Sidhe had called into Balor's Hollow, summoned to his evil bidding and drawn to himself for her destruction. She took it into herself and kept taking, kept breathing in until her lungs ached. And still she breathed in, until all the magic in that place, all the power of enchantment, was imprisoned inside her.

Then all was silence.

The Dark Lord stood dumbfounded, all his magical energy stripped away.

'How—?' he began; and then he roared, an enraged bellow of frustration and fury. 'No! *You* are nothing! *You* are no one! While *I* am Lord over all the Dark Sidhe! I *will* be King in Faery!' He had completely lost control; a frenzy of anger possessed him. 'And I will kill you with my bare hands!' His reason gone, consumed by rage, he hurled himself at her.

The onlookers gasped and Granny O'Hara started forward; but Bansi O'Hara reached up as the Dark Lord's hands came down and seized them in the grip of her own small fingers.

Inside her, the captured fires of enchantment blazed, somehow feeding her physical strength; and with an effort, she held him. He was caught in the grip of madness now and stronger for it, but the magical forces she held inside filled her with an energy she had never known, and she wrestled him to a standstill. They stood, the Dark Lord and the mortal girl, hands and eyes locked together, trapped in a deadly stalemate.

And then she felt the fires within her burning out of control, bubbling, boiling over like molten lava. She tried to damp them down, rein them in; but they pushed up all the more. There was a bad taste in her mouth that spoke of the destruction she would unleash if she released the power from inside her, and she fought to hold it back. Her muscles tensed still further, her eyes bulged with the effort.

The Dark Lord saw her struggle. He pressed his advantage and bore down on her with all his weight. She summoned her strength, held him off, forced him away. Within her the mystical energies exulted like living creatures tasting freedom, as her attention was drawn from them and her hold on them slipped. She strained against her enemy, while inside her mind she focused on the magic and drove it back down. But it resisted her, pushing its way up again, and the dark Lord pushed against her, and she knew the strength to hold them both would not last.

She dropped to her knees; heard her granny gasp. Her friends! Whatever happened, she must save them. But the powers were working against her more than for her now; she could not contain them. She could not protect her companions much longer; but perhaps something else could.

'The car!' she yelled. 'Get in the car!'

They hesitated for only a moment; after what they'd seen her do in the last few minutes, trusting her without question seemed the only option. Granny and the two brownies flung themselves into the Morris Minor without delay, the raven fluttering in behind them, and pressed their faces to the window. Mrs Mullarkey kept her eyes on Conn as she backed towards the car, but as she moved away he rose to his feet and began to stalk her, keeping out of reach of the jack handle. She jabbed at him; he leaped sideways and began to harry her. She jabbed at him again; but he was crafty, like a wolf in pursuit of a stray lamb.

'Mrs Mullarkey!' Bansi cried desperately. 'Get in the car!'

The old woman tried; but Conn was there, between her and the vehicle, keeping just out of range.

A sudden motion, and Tam was there, too,

clinging weakly to Conn's back. Conn shook him off, but Tam caught his ankle as he fell, and held on. 'Go!' he shouted.

'But—' Mrs Mullarkey began.

'Go!' Tam yelled again, as Conn kicked him loose. He clutched once more at the wolf-boy's leg; somehow managed to trip him and hold on. 'It'd kill me getting in there – too much steel! Go!'

'But—' Mrs Mullarkey said again; and then realized he was right. Before Conn could free himself, she hurled herself through the back doors, pulling them closed behind her.

And Bansi stopped pushing, and set the magic free.

Chapter Twenty-Seven

Bansi smiled. And her smile became brighter, and brighter, and brighter, until it was like staring at the sun.

A wave – no, a tide, a storm, a hurricane – of energy broke from her, as all the magical forces she had held inside were suddenly and violently released. It rolled out across Balor's Hollow, its dazzling intensity swallowing the Lord of the Dark Sidhe, gulping down Conn and Tam as they fought, roiling and churning wildly around the dark green Morris Minor Traveller as though trying to burn it away. It enveloped the standing stones with a glowing brilliance, swept on out to the wall-like cliffs, and surged upwards, forcing its way skywards like a great beacon of warning.

In the car, Bansi's companions hid their eyes from the brightness.

On a nearby peak the brownie tribe, revelling in their victory as they watched the Dark Lord's followers flee for their lives into the valley below, fell silent as they turned to see the night sky above Balor's Hollow light up. They drew closer together for comfort, their newfound bravery almost deserting them. At length, one small figure hefted his horseshoe uncertainly and strode off towards the now-dying light. After a few seconds, and one by one, the others followed.

And then the blazing light expanded, rolling out across the landscape towards them; and before they had time to turn and flee it caught them, rolled over them like a great tidal wave, and they, too, were consumed.

If you had been there, in the barren basin of Balor's Hollow as that bright ferocious light faded, you would have seen . . .

Nothing.

Nothing but the standing stones, and the desolate, craggy cliffs and the crazed rocky floor.

Of Bansi O'Hara and her companions, of the Lord of the Dark Sidhe and his warrior wolf-boy, there was no sign.

Chapter Twenty-Eight

The shining, bright white light seemed now to come from within her, from her soul, through her hands and her eyes. It flowered and blossomed like a silent explosion, wiping out Balor's Hollow with its grim standing stones and dark shadows, its history of violence and death and its cruel memories of pain and betrayal. For a moment, its clean stark brightness was all there was.

When it faded, the stone circle still stood around them; but the cliffs were gone. The early morning sun was shining cheerfully down, and a large oak tree stood high above them.

It took Bansi a moment to realize that she was standing in that other stone circle, on the hillside above the sleepy village of Ballyfey.

Everyone was staring at her. The entire brownie tribe – caught up in that last, roiling wave of light – dropped to their knees in reverence. Granny and Mrs Mullarkey, followed by Pogo and Moina, were climbing shakily from the car, open-mouthed in amazement.

'Um . . . how exactly did you do that, love?' Granny asked hesitantly.

'I . . . I don't think it was me,' Bansi began uncertainly, but before she could continue she was interrupted by an excited Pogo.

'Of course it was you!' he cried, dancing around in a most undignified manner. 'You returned the Blood of the Morning Stars to the sacred earth! The inheritance of Derga is yours, Bansi! You've inherited the power of your bloodlines!' He stopped, suddenly aware of the surprised, amused eyes of his tribe fixed on him. 'And . . . and you'd better learn to control it a bit better!' he added gruffly. 'Getting yourselves home was one thing, but bringing me and my whole tribe? No one asked you to do that, did they?'

A ripple of laughter spread amongst the brownies, and Moina, who had joined them where they knelt, leaped to her feet.

'Ignore him, Bansi,' she said, smiling. 'You know what he's like! But know this, too: you have given us dignity. You bear with honour the bloodlines of the Morning Stars of Tir na n'Óg, and you are the true inheritor of their father, Derga. So this tribe now and for ever pledges itself to your service, as we would have done to the Morning Stars themselves.'

As one, the whole tribe rose to their feet and bowed deeply. Then, silently and instantly, they slipped away into the long grass on the hillside, and only Pogo was left.

'Hang on!' Bansi exclaimed; but the brownies were gone. 'How are they going to get home?' she asked Pogo in sudden concern. 'Don't say I've stranded you all here? Won't the gate have closed by now?'

'Ah, I wouldn't worry,' he said, with a quick glance at the sky. 'Time moves differently in the Other Realm. Here, it's still Midsummer Day – only a couple of hours after we left. We can pass through the gate this evening at twilight, before it closes, and I dare say we can keep busy till then. There'll be plenty to do round here, I can tell you. Aye, well . . . better be going myself, I suppose . . .'

Bansi felt a sudden rush of affection for the little man who had been so loyal to her. She dropped to her knees in front of him and took his hands.

'Thank you, Pogo,' she said.

Pogo blushed a deep burgundy. 'Might have been better if you'd never met me,' he muttered. 'I might've got you killed, falling for that trick of Tam's. Still can't believe it of him, you know.'

There was a twist of sorrow in Bansi's heart at the mention of Tam's name. 'I know . . . I really think he wanted to do the right thing, though. I mean – I think he thought he *was* doing the right thing . . . or at least, the least wrong thing. Poor Tam. I wonder what happened to him?'

The little brownie shook his head sadly. 'Maybe I shouldn't speak ill of him. That – whatever-you-did, I've never known magic like it. No one could have survived that, without the protection of iron. I doubt we'll ever see Tam again. I doubt there's much of him left to see . . .'

Time moves differently in the Other Realm; so it may have been just then, or earlier, or later, or all three at once, that a flock of wild goats, grazing in the forest, came upon a young boy, face down and apparently unconscious. Curious, they began to nibble at his hair, and at the tattered, flame-coloured clothing that covered him.

The boy groaned, startling the animals into stepping back. His eyes flickered open and he regarded them with some confusion for a moment.

Then he grinned: a wide grin, full of mischief and – you might have said, had you been there to see it – relief. And then, somehow, he was no longer there. In his place, another goat, slightly larger than the others and with luminous yellow eyes, tottered to its feet.

Being themselves creatures of Faery, the goats were not perturbed. They followed the new goat to see where he would lead them.

'Poor Tam,' Bansi murmured again.

'Maybe. You won't catch me shedding any tears for him, though. Not after what he did.'

'Aye, well, so,' came a familiar voice from behind the oak tree. 'But . . . here! What about thish key, eh? Seein' as I kept her safe an' all . . .'

'Flooter!' Bansi exclaimed. 'How did you—?' In time, she stopped herself, knowing what the answer would be.

Pogo scowled. 'What are you doing here, you drunken fool?' he muttered.

'Ah, Pogo,' Flooter said cheerily, wobbling into view. 'Sure, and aren't I one of your merry band, now?'

'You are not!' Pogo insisted. 'You're just a red-nosed buffoon who keeps turning up like a bad penny!'

'But he did save my life,' Bansi pointed out. 'Thank you, Flooter.'

The cluricaun beamed redly, and offered a wobbly bow. 'Well, now, thank you. And about this key . . . ?'

'What's this key he keeps blathering on about?' asked Granny.

Flooter grinned. 'The key to the wee girl'sh wine cellar, of course! Pogo said I could have it if I kept her safe!'

Pogo scowled. 'I never did,' he said. 'You were the only one going on about a key. What would a child be doing with a wine cellar?'

Flooter's face fell. 'Wha'? But . . . but . . . you mean . . . You said . . . she said . . . Aw, that'sh not fair, sho it isn't! I mean . . . I mean . . .'

'Well,' broke in Mrs Mullarkey, 'I for one don't care whether you were after a reward or not, Mr Flooter. You saved Bansi when none of the rest of us could, and a reward is what you deserve. Tonight there'll be a bottle of the best whiskey I can find sitting on my doorstep for you.'

'Whiskey?' Flooter's eyes lit up. 'Aw, missus, thanksh! Fantashtic! Wey-*hey*!'

And then, without any of them really seeing how, he just wasn't there any more.

'Does he know where you live, then?' Granny asked her friend curiously.

Pogo shook his head. 'Probably not,' he said, 'but he'll find it.'

'No one knows how the cluricaun travel,' Bansi added, 'not even the cluricaun – but wherever they're going, they seem to get there OK. Or at least Flooter does.'

'And we should be going, too,' Granny observed.

'Oh, that's right,' came a voice just above her. 'Don't worry about me; it's not as if *I* helped or anything, after all!' They looked up; the raven was perching on a low branch, looking at them with one beady eye.

Bansi smiled. 'I wondered where you'd got to!' she said. 'You *did* help – hugely. Thank you.'

The raven spread its wings and hopped off the branch. 'Oh, *thank you*,' it echoed bitterly, landing gracefully at her feet. '*Thank you* is a great help.'

'Well, what are you after?' Granny enquired. 'I'm sure Nora would be happy to run over a hedgehog for you, if that'd do.'

The raven tilted its head and glared at her. 'Hedgehogs!' it spat. 'That's all I've got to look forward to for the next five hundred years, isn't it? Only . . .' It turned back to Bansi and paused, with uncharacteristic shyness – or perhaps apprehension. 'Only . . . I was wondering . . . well, if you've got all this power now . . . the power of the Morning Stars . . . I just thought maybe you could turn me back?' it finished in a rush. 'Please?' Pleadingly, it looked up at Bansi and waited.

Bansi didn't know what to say. She looked to the two old ladies for help, but neither spoke; Granny just beamed at her lovingly and proudly, and Mrs Mullarkey's face was impassive and unreadable. She knelt down in front of the bird. 'I don't know if I can,' she said and hesitantly reached out, cupping the bird's skull with one hand. 'But I'll try.'

She closed her eyes. For many seconds, she saw nothing. Then, slowly, a picture began to take shape in her head – a face, indistinct at first, but slowly becoming clear. It was small, delicate and pointed; and it had features which should have been merry but were simply sad and weary. Instinctively, her mind reached out towards it.

Suddenly, and without warning, it was sucked away. Her eyes jerked open with shock; it felt as if a thick rubber band had been snapped harshly against her insides.

Somewhere in the Other Realm, a ragged figure lying on a rough mat in a dark corner of a simple hut suddenly opened his snake-like yellow eyes. Seconds later, he jolted sharply upright as if he had been stung.

'Easy, master,' came a voice from by the fire.

'You're safe here, whoever you are. I found you out on the mountain. Attacked by something, were you?'

The Lord of the Dark Sidhe ignored the speaker and pressed his hands to his head. Somewhere – though where, he couldn't tell – a power was challenging his. It was a great power, that much he could judge; perhaps greater even than his own, though in the hands of one who had not yet learned how to wield it. Still, whatever magic it was trying to undo had held firm.

He closed his eyes wearily and lay back on the mat.

The raven was still looking up at Bansi hopefully. She closed her eyes and tried again, but now she saw nothing. The voices that had seemed to guide her in Balor's Hollow were silent and would not be summoned.

'I'm sorry,' she said, opening her eyes again and looking down at the bird. 'I can't – I don't know how. If I could . . . If I ever learn how I can . . .'

The raven sighed. 'Aw, well,' it croaked sadly, 'you tried. Right, go on, then,' it added with forced jollity, 'go on home before your parents miss you. Don't worry about me! I'll just sit in this tree here for another five hundred years. I'm sure I'll get used to it . . . Not the squashed hedgehogs, though,' it added gloomily. 'Don't think I'll ever get used to the squashed hedgehogs.'

Flapping its wings, it flew off towards the main road.

'Well,' Pogo said. 'Well, now. The day's not getting any younger, and there's lots to do before twilight. Though come to think of it,' he added, as if surprising himself with the thought, 'now the prophecy's been fulfilled . . . *then shall the power of Tir na n'Óg awaken*, it says. *Then shall the ways between the worlds reopen*. In all the worry about the inheritance of Derga, we never even thought about those promises! And I promise you this, Bansi O'Hara,' he added with sudden formality. 'If that ability is returned to us – if all the people of Faery can once again visit the mortal realms with ease – then I shall be watching over you, to protect you with my life if necessary.'

Bansi knelt then, and kissed him gently on the forehead. 'Thank you, Pogo,' she said, 'for everything.'

Again the little man blushed russet. 'It's I who should thank you,' he muttered. 'Farewell then, for now. Oh, aye,' he added, 'and you, you pair of daft old bats.' Then he was gone; although as he vanished into the long grass they clearly heard him mutter, 'Wee girls selling biscuits, indeed! Huh!'

Then they were alone, and it suddenly felt to

Bansi very much as if it had all been a dream. She stared at the bright blue sky above her for a moment and then, with an effort and a very deep breath, turned to Granny and Mrs Mullarkey.

'Did it really happen?' she asked, blinking.

Granny laughed, a laugh born of relief as much as merriment. 'It did, love. Strange as it seems, it all happened. And if you ever should doubt it – well, I've kept a wee souvenir to remind you.' She smiled. 'You could make it into a nice warm pair of slippers, maybe – or a furry cushion cover . . .'

On a wild rocky shore of Tir na n'Óg, a cold wave broke roughly over the prone form of a boy dressed in ripped and torn animal skins. The shock of the cold water startled him from unconsciousness; instinctively, his hand went to the back of his neck, as though checking for something. There was nothing there.

He rose, looked over his shoulder, and howled; a wild, savage howl of bereft rage.

Bansi stroked the coarse fur for a moment, remembering. Then she turned towards the car.

'Come on,' she said, 'let's go home.'

Chapter Twenty-Nine

If you had been there, on the narrow road into Ballyfey, early on that bright midsummer morning, you would certainly have leaped for your life as the Morris Minor Traveller tore through the hedgerow at the bottom of the hill and, with a screech of tyres, slewed round madly to aim itself like a dark green missile at the village.

And had you followed its route around the bend, you would have been most surprised – only moments after the roar of the engine and the sound of two elderly ladies screaming their heads off at each other had faded into the distance – to hear the prickly hawthorn hedge apparently dialling a number.

Then came a muffled cursing, and a sound like someone's shirt being torn by thorns, and the hedge said, 'Hello? Is that you, love? Listen, whatever you do, don't go out of the house today. That mad old bat's done something to her car! It's practically flying! She must be doing a hundred and fifty at least!'

There was a pause. 'What do you mean, the house is all tidy?'

And indeed, all over Ballyfey, people were waking to find not only their houses tidy but their laundry washed, their clocks and televisions and bicycles mended, their neglected shelves at last put up. All day it continued, with villagers finding their chores done after turning their backs for only a moment; and it would continue until just before sunset when, as mysteriously as it had started, the outbreak of housework suddenly came to an end. The letters page of the local paper would be full for weeks afterwards with readers competing to put forward the craziest theories in explanation: aliens; repentant burglars trying to make amends; over-enthusiastic boy scouts; and even, ludicrously, the suggestion from one reader that the village had been invaded by brownies, trying to make up in a single day for a long absence from the world of mortals – although nobody took *that* one seriously for a minute.

The drive home passed in a blur: almost literally, for it seemed that the brownies had worked on the engine as well as the bodywork, and Mrs Mullarkey had never achieved such speeds before. On the seat beside her, Bansi found the jack handle which had saved them so many times in Balor's Hollow; and she clutched it like a talisman all the way back.

'Well, here we are,' Mrs Mullarkey announced minutes later – though to Bansi they were the longest minutes in the world – as the dark green Morris Minor Traveller, kicking up gravel, screeched to a halt outside Granny O'Hara's house. 'By the way, Eileen,' she added, as Granny opened the door and got out to lift the seat forward for Bansi, 'I'll have my pension back – and yours, while you're at it.'

'What?' Granny was scandalized once more. 'Nora, the bet was settled! There's nothing of the changeling about my Bansi, and the money's mine!'

'Nothing of the changeling, perhaps,' Mrs Mullarkey was saying as Bansi, still clutching the jack handle, squeezed out, 'but something of the Good People – which is what I said in the first place, you'll recall. I mean, she's practically queen of a whole tribe of brownies, now!'

'Oh-ho, and I thought there was no such thing as brownies, Nora Maura Margaret Whatever-your-other-name-is Mullarkey? I thought you said they were just wee girls who go round selling biscuits!'

'Eileen! Be fair, now! You lost the bet good and proper! She's descended from the Good People on both sides, she has the blood of their royalty running through her veins, and if *that* wasn't enough, she's inherited some kind of magical powers from them too, and who knows what that'll lead to, by the way – we'll probably both wake up tomorrow turned into frogs or some such . . .'

'Yes, but the bet was about whether she was a changeling . . .'

'Oh no it wasn't!'

'Oh yes it was, Eileen!'

'It was *not*, you barmy old codfish . . . !'

Bansi heard no more. The front door was unlocked; she ran in, hardly noticing how astonishingly clean and tidy the whole place was, and made for the kitchen. It was empty – spotless and gleaming, but uninhabited.

'Mum! Dad!' she called. Her parents must be frantic with worry by now, she suddenly realized; they'd probably called the police, or—

They weren't in the incredibly orderly lounge, either. Bansi hurled herself up the stairs as fast as her legs would carry her, and threw open their bedroom door.

There she stopped, horrified for a second. The room looked just as she'd seen it the previous night – overturned and in chaos, the window smashed, the bed empty. It suddenly occurred to her that Tam might have lied; perhaps her parents *had* been taken, and were even now in the hands of the Dark Sidhe.

Or perhaps not. She took a deep breath, tightened her grip on the jack handle, and stepped across the threshold.

The enchantment dissolved. The room was as neat and in order as the rest of the house; and there, as quiet and serene as two slumbering babies, were her mum and dad, breathing deeply and comfortably under the cosy duvet.

Her mother half opened one beautiful but bleary eye. 'Hello, my darling!' she mumbled. 'Is it the morning already? Did you have a nice sleep?'

Sleep! The realization came upon her that she'd hardly slept at all – she'd been awake for most of the night and then, although it seemed only a few hours had passed here, for a whole long day in the Other Realm.

Sudden weariness fell upon Bansi O'Hara as the events of the day and night overtook her at last. Her eyelids drooped, burning with tiredness. She kicked off her shoes, dropped the jack handle, and climbed onto the bed, snuggling down between her parents. They felt warm and soft and – more wonderful than anything else – they were simply *there*. Her dad smiled sleepily and draped his arm over her; her mum laid her hand softly on Bansi's cheek; both of them sighed contentedly.

Oblivious to either the vigilant brown eyes that

watched over her from the shadows, or the squabbling of the two old ladies downstairs, Bansi O'Hara closed her eyes, cuddled into her parents, and fell fast and peacefully asleep.

About the faery beings named in Bansi O'Hara and the Bloodline Prophecy

As Bansi's chronicler, I have attempted to find out as much as I can about the various faery types mentioned in her adventures. Some of the information below comes from a combination of Bansi's own accounts and my reading of a great number of websites on the faery folk, all easy to find using a search engine and to whose compilers I am indebted. Pronunciation help is given in square brackets.

Annis, the Hag of the Dark Glen: a hag is a faery who takes the shape of an old woman. Many hags in legend are, like Annis, flesh-eaters with a particular preference for the taste of human children; the witch in the story of *Hansel and Gretel* was probably a hag.

Brownies: Pogo, Moina and their tribe belong to a race best known from Scottish legend. The brownie is generally a helpful faery who works in secret – usually at night – to tidy mortal dwellings. They do not expect a reward of any sort, and will usually leave the house if one is offered.

Brúid:*(Broo-id)*:creatures like Brúid, shaped like headless humans, with facial features located on or around the torso and with a taste for human flesh, are best known from English folklore.

Caithne: *(Ca-hnee; the 'h' is not silent)* **of the Sacred Grove**: a **dryad**, a creature best known from Greek mythology.

Changelings: Irish and British folklore is full of reports of the faery folk stealing away human babies and replacing them with changelings. These beings have the ability to disguise themselves as the mortal child whose place they take. If the changeling can be tricked into revealing that it is not mortal, it must then go back to the Other Realm, and the human child will be returned to its proper home.

Cluricaun: **Flooter** belongs to a faery people notorious in Irish myth for their drinking habits. They are probably closely related to the leprechaun; some sources believe them to be the same creature relaxing after a hard day's work. Whichever the case, you will never meet a sober cluricaun. They will sometimes mount dogs or sheep as if they were horses and take them on wild midnight rides.

Conn: There are many tales in Celtic legend of faery folk who change shape by donning or doffing an animal-skin, most famously the *selkie* (or seal-people) of the Orkneys, or the *swan-maidens* of Irish legend. There are ancient Irish stories of mortals who wander into the Other Realm and encounter wolves there; it is possible some of these may have been not true wolves but skin-changers like Conn.

Púca, Tam: a powerful but often mischievous faery creature from Irish legend. In some areas they are best known for appearing in the form of a goat; in others as a great black horse with burning yellow eyes.

Sidhe *(shee)*: The Sidhe are an ancient and powerful faery race, sometimes identified with the Tuatha de Danaan, a magical people who according to legend ruled over ancient Ireland. In common with most faery folk, they are indifferent to the fate of mortals, seeing them as of little consequence, and can be kindly or cruel as the mood takes them. There are many sub-groups of sidhe, the most famous being the banshee (or *bean sidhe*), and for this reason the term is occasionally used to encompass all faery folk.

Tir na n'Óg *(Teer na n'Ogue – to rhyme with rogue)* means *the Land of Youth,* but may properly also be referred to as the Other Realm or the Land of Faery. According to legend, in ancient times it was not uncommon for wanderers to find themselves in Tir na n'Óg, which for some was a wonderful adventure and for others was terrible indeed. Time runs differently there; there are some stories of mortals who believed they had spent as little as a single night in the Other Realm, but who returned home to find that months, years, or even a century had passed.

ABOUT THE AUTHOR

When John Dougherty was little, he wanted to be a superhero, but somehow he became a primary school teacher instead – which isn't quite the same thing. Then he became an author, and now he has lots of fun visiting schools to talk about his work. He is also a performing singer-songwriter and occasional poet.

John's first book for young readers, *Zeus on the Loose*, was shortlisted for the Branford Boase Award in 2005, while his second, *Niteracy Hour*, was shortlisted for the Nottinghamshire Children's Book Award.

He lives in Stroud, Gloucestershire, with his wife and two children.

www.visitingauthor.com

JOHN DOUGHERTY

Jack Slater
Monster Investigator

'MMM, YUM YUM! Eat children! Yeah!'

Jack Slater is the world's greatest Monster Investigator. He'd like to see a monster get the better of him. But now something BIG is afoot. Which means just one thing . . . Jack must arm himself with his penlight torch and trusty teddy and go down to the monster underworld – before it's too late.

The question is: do the monsters feel lucky . . . ?

'A clever story, cleverly told' *Carousel*

'Dougherty writes superbly . . . a fabulously monstrous novel' www.writeaway.co.uk

'A terrific, funny fantasy' *Julia Eccleshare on* www.lovereading4kids.com

'Clever plotline . . . jokes and intriguing characters' *Children's Books, Ireland*

ISBN 978 0 552 55372 8

www.kidsatrandomhouse.co.uk